dark ESCORT

book three of the beautiful entourage series

E. L. TODD

Fallen Publishing

Dark Escort

Cover Design provided by Dinoman Designs

Copyright © 2015 by E. L. Todd

All Rights Reserved

SBN-13: 978-1511910781

ISBN-10: 151191078X

Cato & Katarina

prologue

Cato

New York City was the greatest damn place on earth.

The food was awesome, the bars were always open, and the chicks were hot. I'd never live anywhere else as long as I lived. And Manhattan was the place to be for my favorite holiday. Technically, it wasn't really a holiday, but it was a holiday to me.

New Year's Eve.

The streets were crowded with people. Confetti was flying through the air even though the ball hadn't dropped, people were bundled up under coats and scarves because it was bone-chilling cold, and most of the people were already drunk.

The best thing about this holiday was the resolutions. Women were always doubting themselves and thinking they were leading their lives in a bad way. Chicks even broke up with their boyfriends because they wanted to start the New Year right. They were adventurous and would do things they'd never done before.

Basically, it was the easiest day of the year to get laid.

Jett, River, and I moved through the crowd so we could find a good spot.

"My dick is so frozen it's going to fall off," Jett muttered. He wore gloves on his hands and his breath was escaping in wisps.

"Suck it up," River said as he punched him in the arm. "I can't believe Troy and Rhett bailed."

"Sitting at home and watching the ball drop on TV is pretty pathetic," I agreed. Union Square was right in their backyard and they didn't even appreciate it. Why did people have to stop living their lives once they settled down? I would never end up like that.

"So, who are our dates for the evening?" River said as he scoped the crowd.

"Yeah," Jett said. "Who are we going to sleep with then ditch first thing in the morning?"

I looked around and tried to find a chick that wasn't completely drowning in a huge jacket and boots. Then I zoned in and found a group of three girls. I wasn't sure if they were all pretty because only one had my attention.

The brunette was short, just a little over five feet, but she made her presence known with her obvious beauty. She held herself like she respected herself, and her eyes twinkled like icicles hanging from the outside of an igloo.

She was definitely a looker.

A gray beanie sat on her head, and her curled hair trailed on either side of her face. She wore a blood red pea coat, and her cheeks were rosy from the cold. She looked up at the sky, amazed by the sight of falling confetti and twinkling lights hanging from the rooftops.

I stared at her for so long I forgot the noise of the crowd. Even my boys' voices fell on deaf ears.

"Check out the fresh meat," River said. "They sure are cute."

"I got the brunette," Jett said immediately.

"I got the girl in the red jacket!" I shouted.

"No, I called her," Jett said.

"Forget it," I argued. "Take the blonde."

"I don't like blondes," Jett argued.

"Hey," River wrapped his arms around our shoulders. "When the lights are off and you can't see a thing, what does it really matter?" A smug grin was on his face and his eyes sparkled in mischief.

Jett and I both looked at each other.

"I still get her," I argued.

"Don't be a dick," Jett snapped.

"I'm going for it." I headed over there.

"Jackass." Jett's voice came from behind me.

"I'll take any of them," River said. "They're all cute."

I got to Red Jacket first, and I tried to be sly about it. If I ran trying to beat Jett I'm pretty sure it would freak her out. I wore a long sleeve shirt and a jacket but I didn't wear a beanie or a hat. I wanted my face to be clear and visible.

Red Jacket turned to me once she noticed me. Her lips was turned in a slight smile like she was amused, but her eyes were guarded because I was a random stranger that just walked up to her.

"What's your New Year's Resolution?" I asked. "And please don't tell me it's to lose weight."

The hesitation disappeared from her eyes once she recognized my charm. She looked into my blue eyes, clearly liking what she saw, and then a beautiful smile broke out on her lips. "To try every different kind of Oreo."

I heard a lot of New Year's resolutions, like taking more pictures, spending more time with friends, learning a new skill, whatever. But I never heard that one before. "You know, that has to be the best one I've ever heard."

"Really?" She seemed a little surprised.

"Definitely."

"What's yours?" she asked.

"Uh...I don't want to say." I kicked my foot out and looked at the ground like I was embarrassed.

"Why not?" She shifted her weight and relaxed, like she was having a good time with me.

"How am I supposed to follow that?" I asked seriously.

Jett reached the group then gave me a distinct and unmistakable glare.

I smiled in a dramatic way, knowing I cock-blocked him good, and then turned back to Red Jacket. "When you open up with something like that how am I supposed to compete?"

"It's not a competition."

"Life is a competition," I said. "Whether we want to admit it or not."

Her eyes reflected the lights from above. "Just tell me. I won't make fun of you."

I shrugged. "To lose weight."

She got my joke and laughed loudly.

I smiled while I listened to her. It was such a cute laugh. It was loud but it was also controlled. She even snorted a little.

"Seriously, what is it?"

"To run the Boston Marathon."

She eyed my body up and down, not being discreet about it. Then she faced me again. "You don't strike me as a runner..."

"Because...?"

"You're so...muscular."

I smiled, showing her my full set of teeth. "Why, thank you. But I enjoy running as well as lifting tree logs and bulldozers."

She nodded, clearly entertained. "I didn't realize you were the Hulk."

"Well, I'm not the original one. But he had to retire sometime."

She laughed again.

I had some slick moves.

The guys talked to their dates, and the girls seemed to like them. Of course they did. When did girls not like us? We were rich and good-looking. If we combined the number of girls we slept with, we would give prostitutes a run for their money.

"What's your name?" I asked.

She didn't answer because she looked at something over my shoulder. "The ball is about to drop."

I looked at the time. There was a minute left on the clock. Then I turned back to her. "Your lips have a date in the next minute?"

She gave me a playful smile. "I need to check my calendar."

"Someone's popular…"

She shrugged in guilt.

"Well, can you cancel your plans? Because my lips are going for it anyway."

She swayed from side to side while she rested one finger on her chin. "Hmm…"

"Oh, the anticipation."

She finally decided. "You're really cute, so okay."

"You're cute too." I came closer to her and got ready for the ball to drop.

The other guys seemed to be kissing their girls at midnight too.

I kissed a different stranger every year on New Year's. It was an odd tradition I had.

"10…" She watched the big clock.

"9…" I said.

Her shoulder was pressed to mine and she looked at me in excitement, like she couldn't wait to get her lips on me.

"You ready for this?" I asked playfully.

"The question is, are you ready for me?" Confidence was in her eyes.

"I guess I'll find out."

The ball finally dropped, and the new year had arrived. The crowd cheered and threw their hats in the air. Confetti dropped and sprinkled around us. It was freezing but everyone seemed to forget that for a moment.

My hand moved around her waist, and the action made me realize how petite she was. She was at least five inches shorter than me, so I had to lean down and get access to her lips. Her arms immediately wrapped around my neck and she closed the distance between us with enthusiasm.

I went for a closed-mouth kiss first so I wouldn't be too forward. Her lips were soft like I expected, and even though I was kissing a stranger it didn't feel foreign. Actually, it felt familiar.

When she didn't pull away, I kissed her hard, massaging her lips with mine. It turned into a make-out session, but since she was cool with it I kept going. Her lips danced around mine like she was a professional, and her tongue slowly made its way into my mouth.

I pulled her into my chest harder then grabbed the back of her neck, deepening the kiss and falling hard into her embrace. I was a bit old-fashioned when it came to kissing. I really enjoyed it and thought it could be hotter than sex sometimes.

She was definitely a good kisser.

I wanted to keep going but she pulled away. "We'll be out here all night..." She tucked a strand of hair behind her ear but there was a sense of playfulness in her eyes.

I stared at her lips, wanting to kiss her again. "That'd be a shame." A note of sarcasm was in my voice. I'm sure she picked up on it.

When I looked passed her shoulder, I realized my boys were gone. They obviously hooked up with their ladies. It was okay to ditch a friend if getting laid was involved. "Your girlfriends are gone."

She turned and looked. "Why doesn't that surprise me?"

"Well, I don't have any plans for the rest of the evening." I gave her my best smoldering look.

"You want to spend it with me?"

"After that kiss, fuck yeah I do."

Her cheeks flushed with pink. "What did you have in mind?"

I had one thing on my mind. "First, let's get a drink. Then let's start that New Year's resolution. You need to try all the different kinds of Oreos."

She laughed, and the joy reached her eyes. "Right now?"

"If not now, when?"

***

We went to a convenient store then migrated to the cookie aisle. When we found the Oreos I was surprised there were so many different flavors. "I didn't know they had different choices. I always get the regular ones."

She stood by my side and looked at the shelves. "You don't look like you munch on cookies all day."

An involuntary smile spread on my lips. "Everything in moderation."

She grabbed mint, vanilla, and root beer flavors.

"Root beer?" I asked. "I doubt that would even taste good."

"We're about to find out."

After we paid for the Oreos we headed outside and stopped on the sidewalk. She grabbed the box on mint flavor Oreos then took a bite. She chewed slowly with a concentrated look in her eyes. "Hmm...pretty good."

I grabbed one and shoved it into my mouth. "Not bad. Reminds me of mint chip ice cream."

She opened the vanilla box then tried one. "It's okay."

I did the same. "Not my favorite."

Then she opened the root beer package. "I'm really hesitant about this one."

I eyed the box then her. "Dido."

"You go first." She handed me the box.

"What if it's poisoned?"

She shrugged. "I'll call an ambulance."

I chuckled. "How sweet of you." I ripped open the plastic then shoved one into my mouth. Then I made a pleasant face and moaned. "Wow, they're really good."

"Really?" Disbelief was in her voice.

"These are my favorite." I handed the box to her.

She immediately took one out and took a bite. Then her face contorted in disgust and she spit it out.

"Gotcha."

She wiped her mouth then shook her head when she faced me. "Gross..."

I laughed as she shook head quickly with pursed lips. "You shouldn't have made me go first."

She smacked me on the arm playfully. "You're such a jerk."

"Hey, you had to try it anyway, right?"

"Even so…" She threw everything in the garbage. "That's the quickest I've completed a New Year's resolution."

"Mine will take a while."

"Well, we could go running now…" She scrunched up her face like that idea wasn't even somewhat pleasing.

"I have a better idea." I pushed her up against the store window then sealed my mouth over hers. As soon as our lips moved together, her hands moved to my upper arms and she gripped them tightly, like she loved what I was doing to her. Our tongues danced together, and everything else seemed to fade to the background. A bum was sitting just a few feet from us, but he'd probably seen worse.

My hand fisted her hair and I pulled her head back, exposing more of her mouth. I breathed deeply into her then moved my lips along her jaw to her ear. My light kisses made her moan, and I continued down her neck while I continued to grip her. Then I moved back to her mouth as my hand moved up her shirt and jacket and groped her breasts over the bra.

Her desire increased at the touch, and she purposely grinded against my definition in my jeans.

My hand moved under the bra and I pinched her nipple slightly then rubbed my thumb across it, making it pebble. She gasped into my mouth then dug her nails into my skin.

She abruptly ended the kiss, her eyes filled with stars. "Want to head to your place?"

I didn't like bringing chicks to my apartment because I couldn't slip out the next morning while she slept. But I really liked this girl. She was an awesome kisser and she was a cool person. I'd encountered a lot of strangers and created a conversation out of thin air, but never so fluidly. She and I just clicked from the beginning. After I slept with her, I'd probably want to sleep with her again. I wasn't totally against relationships. I'd just never met a girl I wanted to have a relationship with. But maybe she would be different. I liked what I saw so far. "Good idea. The bum is getting a free show."

***

As soon as we wandered into my apartment, the clothes started to come off. I pushed her against the wall as I kissed her and felt her up. We somehow migrated to the couch and my jeans were around my ankles. The more clothes I pulled off of her, the harder I became. She was all curves under that red jacket.

When she was just in her lacy underwear and I was in my boxers, I guided her to my bedroom, knocking over a table along the way.

She released a chuckle. "Oh shit."

"It's from Target. Who cares?" I kept kissing her and moving her to my bedroom. Her skin was soft under my hands, and she smelled like snow mixed with vanilla. Every inch of her tasted wonderful.

I got her on my bed then ripped her thong off.

She looked up at me, desire in her eyes. Her hands moved to my thighs and she squeezed them, beckoning me to her.

I knew we should do foreplay but I was already worked up. I wanted to be inside her and break my bed from thrusting inside her. I wanted her to scratch me so much that I bled.

I kneeled at the end of the bed and pulled her hips to me. I lavished her pussy with kisses, sucking and tasting. She dug her nails into my hair and moaned, quiet screams of pleasure escaping that small mouth.

I pushed her to the edge of an orgasm before I stood up and pulled down my boxers.

She immediately moved to her knees on the floor and took in my length. She opened her mouth wide, unhinging it like a snake, then took me in deep. She sucked my tip before she did it again.

Fuck, she gave good head.

My hand fisted her hair and I guided her further onto my cock. She did such a good job that I didn't want her to stop. Seeing her on her knees and trying to take in as much as she could was sending shivers down my spine. I wanted sex, but when she did such a good job sucking dick I didn't want to stop.

She pulled away then placed a gentle kiss on the tip, looking at me as she did it.

A moan from deep in my throat came out.

Then she moved to her back on the bed.

I watched her, feeling my cock get even harder, and then I moved over her. My hand immediately went to my nightstand where I had more condoms then I would ever need. I took one out then ripped the foil.

She grabbed the condom then did the honors. She pinched the tip then rolled it all the way down to the base. She licked her lips as she did it, like she was just as excited to have him inside her pussy as well as her mouth.

I knew I was in for a treat.

Sometimes one-night stands were a little awkward because we were both tipsy and we were strangers. But it wasn't like that with her. It seemed like I was having sex with an old friend.

I separated her thighs with mine and pinned them back as I leaned over her. My lips found her just as my thick cock slid inside. She was soaked down below, and that allowed me to squeeze in. Her pussy was tight, and my cock loved it. "Fuck..." I moved until I was completely sheathed then I kept kissing her.

Her fingers moved up my back to my shoulders and she dug her nails into the skin, just the way I liked. She released a loud moan that almost came out as a scream. I loved it when girls were loud during sex. It told me when I was doing something right, and when I wasn't doing enough.

I rocked her into my mattress, making the headboard tap against the wall. If my neighbors heard it, they would hate me. But they hadn't complained so far. I was already working up a sweat because I was thrusting into her with everything I had. She used my body as an anchor then rocked into me from below.

Shit, she was hot.

We were fucking like animals, trying to get off and get the other person off at the same time. She didn't just lie there like most girls. She gave me equal effort, sliding onto my cock as I shoved it inside her.

Her head rolled back and she released a deep moan. "God, yes…"

Sweat dripped from my chest onto her breasts, and the sight was a turn on. She already had a built up of moisture between her tits and I liked watching the skin glisten.

Finally, she tightened around me and started to come all over my dick. Screams came from her throat and she dug her nails hard into me. "Yes…yes!" She remained tight around my cock until the orgasm started to fade. Her cheeks were rosy red and her nipples were hard.

Then she grabbed my shoulder and rolled me onto my back. Balancing on the balls of her feet, she held onto my chest and bounced up and down. She had the stamina of a cheetah and she kept going even when she broke out in a sweat. I laid back and enjoyed it. My hands gripped her hips and I felt the deep burn in my gut. I was about to explode and I knew it was going to feel amazing.

"Come for me," she said as she panted.

Those words, uttered in a sexy voice, made me shatter. My entire body tensed and I gripped her hips as I released. She kept going, making it feel amazing until the very last drop was spilled. A groan from deep in my throat came out, and my body relaxed in satisfaction.

She got off of me then lay beside me on the bed.

I stared at the ceiling as I recovered from my high. "Fuck, you're good."

"Right back at you." She caught her breath as she lay beside me.

I grabbed the tissues on my nightstand and cleaned up before I turned off the light and snuggled close to her. I was still warm but I wanted to be next to her at the same time. My arm wrapped around her waist and I felt her back expand with every breath. "Where did you learn to fuck like that?" I said into her ear.

"Porn."

I smirked. "I knew you were my type."

"Just from looking at me?" she asked playfully.

"No. When you said eating Oreos was your New Year's resolution."

"And that told you everything you needed to know?" she said with a chuckle.

I kissed her shoulder. "Yep."

"Interesting..."

"So, are you from New York?" I realized I hadn't asked her anything important beforehand.

She yawned loudly and with exaggeration. Her back pressed into my chest as she did it. "No. I'm from California." Her voice came out quiet, like she was trying not to fall asleep.

"Here for the holidays?" I was a bit disappointed she wasn't from New York. But we could make it work somehow. She would probably be here for another week or so.

"My family lives here..." Her voice was trailing off even more.

I kissed her shoulder again, loving the way her skin tasted when it was mixed with sweat. "What's your name?" I never asked beforehand.

She didn't respond.

I sat up and peered into her face.

Her eyes were closed and her face was relaxed. She was clearly asleep.

I'll just ask in the morning.

***

My eyes were closed but I could feel the sunlight pour on my face. It was warm, and it stirred me from the deep sleep I was in. Automatically, my hand reached out for Red Jacket. I groped the sheets but didn't find her.

My eyes peered open and I searched the bed, squinting so only a limited amount of light could get in. She was nowhere to be seen and I realized I was alone. Perhaps she was in the kitchen or the bathroom. I opened my mouth to call her name but I realized I didn't know what it was. "Uh...baby?" That was a good way to go.

No response.

"Baby?" I called again.

I sighed then got out of bed. Then I noticed the torn piece of paper sitting on my nightstand. I grabbed it and examined it.

Happy New Year. Whenever I eat Oreos, especially the root beer kind, I'll think of you.

-K-

I read the note twice even though it didn't gleam any additional information. The paper was from an envelope sitting on my nightstand. I felt it in my hands, like it would tell me something more.

A sensation started in my stomach but I couldn't identify what it was. I was disappointed, even hurt. She left without saying goodbye to me, without giving me a phone number.

She didn't even tell me her name.

Was this how every girl felt when I slipped out the following morning? Did they always feel like this? Or did I feel this way because I genuinely like this girl? Now I could never find her even if I tried. She lived in California and I didn't even have a name to begin my search. But she clearly didn't want to be found anyway.

I lay back in bed and had no energy to do anything. I remembered my night with her clearly, how our first kiss was filled with chemistry and electricity when the ball dropped. She and I stood outside a convenient store and tried different Oreos then made out in front of a bum. Then we had the best sex I've ever had in my life. Connections like that didn't happen to me very often. It took a lot for a girl to impress me. And when I finally found a girl I wanted to know more about, she ditched me. Perhaps it's what I deserved. Perhaps it was karma.

I felt like shit.

E. L. Todd

Two Years Later...

Cato

I walked into the office then approached Danielle's desk. "Hey, beautiful." I grabbed the folder sitting on her desk then dropped into the seat facing her. I gave her a wink before I opened the folder.

Danielle rolled her eyes, but it was half-asked. She liked it when I hit on her even though she acted like she didn't. There was obvious color in her cheeks, and it picked up her confidence. "Knock it off, Cato." Her voice wasn't stern like it usually was when she was genuinely upset over something. I'd known her long enough to understand the difference.

"What?" I asked innocently. "A guy can't tell a girl she's beautiful anymore?"

"We work together."

"So?" I gave her a smug look. "I can say what I damn well please."

She turned to her computer and couldn't wipe the smirk off her lips. She'd broken up with her boyfriend about three months ago, and her depression was obvious in everything she did. I was just trying to cheer her up without actually telling her what I was doing.

"Do you understand your assignment?" she asked without looking at me.

"You act like I'm a CIA operative."

"You kinda are," she said in a teasing tone.

I flipped through the pages. "Needs a boyfriend to protect her from her family…" I skimmed through the lines. "Pretty typical. This will be easy like it always is."

"You're a pro, Cato," she said vaguely.

"When am I meeting her?"

"Tomorrow at noon. Same place."

I opened the folder and looked at the name. "Katarina…pretty hot name."

She rolled her eyes.

"Danielle is a hot name too," I said quickly.

She laughed. "That wasn't why I rolled my eyes. I don't care about your opinion of what you think is hot."

"Yes, you do…" I winked at her.

She rolled her eyes dramatically. "Get out of here, Cato."

"Yes, Ma'am."

***

I met River at the bar.

"You got your next assignment?" he asked as he drank his beer.

"Yep. Katarina..." I wiggled my eyebrows. "Sounds hot."

"Hopefully she's not for your sake."

"I can keep it in my pants...unlike you."

River rolled his eyes. "It happened one time. You guys need to stop throwing that in my face."

"Let me think about that." I rubbed my chin. "Nah. Too much fun."

He looked like he wanted to punch me in the face but he found the restraint not to. "Had a threesome last night."

"Cool. How'd that go?"

He shrugged. "It was okay."

I cocked an eyebrow and gave him an incredulous look. "A threesome should never be *just okay*. Did you do it wrong?"

"Of course I didn't do it wrong," he argued. "I'm just getting bored."

"What the fuck is wrong with you?" I blurted. "Two women at once should never be boring."

He shrugged. "Maybe I should make it a foursome or something..."

"You could do that."

"But I kinda want to try something different..." He gave me a particular look.

"No fucking way," I snapped. "I'm not doing a threesome with another dude."

E. L. Todd

He flashed me a look of annoyance. "No, idiot. What about a group fuck? Two guys and two girls? That'd be pretty hot."

"You want to watch me have sex with a girl?"

"I'm not going to stare at you the whole time. But it would be something different. We can trade girls too."

"I don't know, man…it might get weird."

"Only if we make it weird." He drank his beer again.

"I thought you were looking for a girl to settle down with anyway?" I asked.

River shrugged. "And have I ever found anyone?" He finished his beer and left the glass on the table. "I officially give up. The right girl isn't out there. There are just…other girls."

"Well, maybe you shouldn't look for Mrs. Right in a bar," I argued. "Try a bookstore or something."

"I don't read, Cato."

"But you can look at picture books," I teased.

"I'm sure the ladies will love that." He leaned forward and lowered his voice. "So, you want to do it or what?"

"I don't know, man."

"Come on, live a little."

I felt the glass in my fingertips. "If I agree to this, we can't tell anyone."

"Why?" he demanded. "The guys will think it's cool."

"That's my condition."

"Fine," he said as he released a sigh. "Whatever."

"Now we have to find the girls."

River winked. "Leave that to me."

***

When I reached the coffee shop, I pulled out the piece of paper with Katarina's information. I hadn't looked at her driver's license yet so I had no idea what she looked like. It would be impossible to find her when I only knew her name.

I examined the picture and squinted. She was a pretty girl with brown hair and bright blue eyes. She looked faintly familiar but I couldn't figure out where I knew her from. The picture could have been taken five years ago. Maybe that was why I couldn't pin her down. I shoved the paper back into my pocket then entered the coffee shop.

The scent of freshly ground beans entered my nose, and the quiet chatter of people came into my ears. I wore slacks and a collared shirt, looking spiffy and professional. I scanned the room and looked for my next client.

My eyes settled on a brunette near the window. A cup of coffee was in front of her along with a blueberry muffin that only had a few bites taken out of it. She wore jeans and a teal top, bringing out her skin tone and eyes. I stilled when she turned my way. Those lips were ingrained in my memory forever. I remembered the way they felt against mine, and I remembered those eyes as they burned when I had her on my bed.

I couldn't believe it was *her*.

It was the girl I met on New Year's two years ago. That night came back to me, and I remembered her unusual resolution to try different Oreos. She left without saying goodbye, and I woke up feeling like shit.

What were the odds of this happening?

The only information I had about her was the fact she lived in California.

So what was she doing here?

I froze, debating whether I should take off just like she did to me. I could have one of the other guys do it. Most of them owed me favors anyway. But I didn't move because she was staring straight at me.

It didn't seem like she knew who I was. That flash of recognition didn't come into her eyes. But how could she not remember me? That hurt even more.

Then she gave me a small smile and waved hesitantly, like she wasn't completely sure if I was the guy she was waiting for.

Don't be a pussy.

I squared my shoulders then approached her table. "Hi." I wasn't as polite and pleasant as I normally was. I guess I hadn't let go of the fact she just bailed on me. Was this how most girls felt toward me?

"Hi." She looked up at me and smiled.

She seriously didn't recognize me? I was pretty damn unforgettable. "Cato." I extended my hand to shake hers. It felt odd since I'd already kissed her and held her. Now it was like that never happened.

"Katarina," she said. "But call me Kat."

"I prefer Katarina." I refused to let her have the power in the conversation. I moved to the seat across from her and rested my ankle on the opposite knee. I kept my back straight and shoulders tense. When I looked at her, a flashback of the way she rode me came into my mind. The sex was fucking mind-blowing.

"Thank you for meeting me today," she said politely. Her teal blouse brought out her eyes, and they looked the same as they had on that night in Times Square. They twinkled even when there were no lights.

She was sweet, just like she used to be. But I didn't like that. "I'm just doing my job."

She didn't seem offended by my slightly hostile behavior. She either didn't pick up on it or just ignored it. "So...I've never done this before and I'm not sure how it works." She looked to me for guidance.

I adopted my professional façade. "Tell me what you need me to do."

"Well..." She looked at her hands in her lap. "It's a long story."

"I have all day." I stared at her face intently and watched her look at me. I waited for her to recognize me, to finally make the connection that I was the one-night stand she had on New Year's Eve two years ago. How did she not remember me? And more importantly, how could she leave me without wanting to see me again? Did she not feel what I felt? This was driving me crazy and I wasn't sure why. My confidence was shaken, and a girl had never done that before.

"Basically, my parents are best friends with another couple they've known forever. They have a son named Joey. He's a really nice guy and he's very handsome, but...he's just not for me. My parents are really pushing me toward him even though I've asked them to stop. The reason why is because my family owns a large winery, and his family owns a large shipping company. If we married, we could combine both worlds. Another problem is, Joey won't stop pursuing me. I think his feelings are more than just political. That's where you come in."

I've heard different iterations of this story countless times.

"I need you to pose as my boyfriend for an indefinite amount of time. Maybe one day they'll accept it's really not going to happen between Joey and I. But the best way to achieve that is to show them I'm in love with someone else."

I nodded my understanding. "Why don't you just get a boyfriend?" It was a personal question but I was entitled to the answer since her personal life was my job.

"Because I don't want a boyfriend," she said simply. "If and when I find the right guy, I'll consider it. But for now, I'm very happy with my life."

There was more to this story but I didn't press her on it. "I understand."

"So, do you think you can help me?"

"Definitely."

"My family is wealthy so they are a bit snooty, fair warning."

"I can be snooty too," I said. "Problem solved."

"Okay," she said. "Is there anything else you need to know?"

Yeah, why the fuck don't you remember me? "No."

"Great," she said. "The winery is hosting a charity event for my father's benefit company. I'd like to make your introduction there. It's black tie."

"Okay."

She rested her hands on the table and regarded me for a moment. "You're easy to work with. This is nice. Honestly, I didn't know what to expect."

"It's a job," I said simply. "I do what you pay me to do. It's that simple."

She nodded. "I heard you were professional but I had no idea just how much."

"You get what you pay for." Would I be able to do this? I couldn't stop being cold toward her. And I found it ironic that she liked my distant attitude. Was this woman made of ice? When we met two years ago, she was happy and upbeat. It was like she was two different people. It didn't make any sense.

"Here's my number." She wrote it down on a napkin. "Call me if you need anything."

"Danielle will speak to you on my behalf." I pushed the number back. "We never speak personally."

"My apologies." She took it back without asking any questions.

Two years ago, I would have loved to have her number and chase her down. Now I pushed it away like it was poison.

She stood up and shouldered her bag. "It was nice meeting you, Cato."

Against my will, I quickly checked her out. She was the same size as before, thin but curvy at the same time. I remembered the way she tasted and how tight her pussy was. Would I ever stop thinking about it when I was around her? I wanted to dig my hand into her hair.

I stood up then shook her hand again. "You too," I forced myself to say. I stared straight into her eyes, waiting for her to make the connection.

Come on, woman.

"I'll be in touch." She gave me a quick smile before she walked away.

I stayed rooted to the spot, unable to believe that just happened.

***

"So let me get this straight," Jett said from his side of the couch. "This is the same girl from New Year's a few years ago? The girl in the red jacket?"

"Yeah." I still couldn't believe it.

"And she doesn't remember you?"

"At all."

He smirked and tried to hide it. "Maybe you weren't that memorable…"

"Don't make me kick your ass."

He laughed and didn't bother to stop himself. "I just can't believe she doesn't remember you. Do you look that different?"

"No. I haven't grown a beard or gained or lost a bunch of weight."

"Maybe this girl is such a slut she can't even remember who she slept with. You're perfect for each other."

"Even then..." I rubbed my chin because I couldn't figure it out.

"Why does it bother you so much?" he asked seriously. "It's not a big deal. It probably makes your life easier anyway."

"I just..." I didn't want to tell him about that night. She left when I was still asleep, and feeling abandoned like that hurt. Ever since then, I hadn't pulled that number on a girl. I frankly told them from the beginning I wouldn't be around in the morning. What goes around comes back around, right?

"What?" Jett asked.

"Yeah, you're right. It's not a big deal."

"Hey, when you fuck her again it'll be fun." He wiggled his eyebrows.

"She's my client now," I reminded him.

"She won't be your client forever."

Katarina

Hiring an escort was something I never thought I would do in a million years. I was perfectly fine being alone, and I always wanted to be alone. Relationships were something I just couldn't handle, and I would never change my mind about that.

Why wouldn't my family understand that?

I was working in my office at home when there was a knock on the door. I stopped typing and wondered who it was. If a friend came by, they usually let me know first. I headed to the peephole then looked through.

Joey was on the other side, wearing jeans and a black t-shirt. It fit him nicely along the chest. He was a nice guy who was respectful and sweet, but sometimes he couldn't take a hint.

I opened the door and plastered a smile on my face. "Hey, what's up?"

His eyes honed in on me, like usual. Trying to be discreet, he examined every inch of me. When his eyes settled on my face, he looked at me like he hadn't seen me in years. I hated the attention he gave me sometimes. I felt like a specimen in a lab being studied. "I was just in the neighborhood and wanted to see if you'd be interested in lunch."

"I actually have a lot of work today."

He gave me that look that told me he thought I was crazy. "It's Saturday."

"And...?"

"Come on, it's just a bite." He gave me a smile, and a dimple formed on each cheek. Joey really was a sweet person. He had classically handsome features. He was tall and broad, and he had a stern jaw with bright eyes. It was clear he hit the gym often, and he was a sweetheart.

But I didn't feel anything.

And I never would.

"You have to eat sometime, right?" he pressed. He put his hands in his pockets and stayed on my doorstep. I was grateful he never tried to hug me or cross the line. He seemed to understand I was off limits unless I specified otherwise.

He wore me down. "Sure, why not?"

"Awesome." He stepped back and waited for me to grab my purse. "What are you in the mood for?"

"Anything."

"Burgers, it is."

***

I picked at my fries then sipped my coke.

He rested his elbows on the table while he shoved the burger into his mouth. He took a large bite like an animal then chewed it slowly. As soon as he had the food in his mouth, he removed his elbows off the table. "Like your food?"

"It's amazing, like always."

"Aren't you glad you came out?"

I gave him a smile. "I suppose."

"If not the food, at least the company." He had a teasing look in his eyes.

"Of course." I ate a few more fries and felt my stomach stretch with fullness.

"What are you working on at home?"

"Just paperwork," I said with a sigh. "It never ends."

"I can tell," he noted.

"How's work for you?"

He shrugged. "The same."

I looked out the window and watched the people walk up the street of Manhattan. Some had shopping bags and others held tall cups of coffee. I absentmindedly played with an earring while I watched them go.

"What are you thinking?" he blurted.

I turned back to him, realizing I drifted. "Sorry, I wasn't really thinking anything."

He finished his food then stared at me. He hardly blinked as he did it. He did this from time to time and I tried to pretend I didn't notice. But he was making it really obvious. I turned to him and faced him head-on.

He held my gaze, confident, and then looked away when he took a drink of his soda.

Sometimes I wondered if he did have feelings for me. He never expressed his annoyance that our parents were trying to put us together. But he never said he wanted it either.

"So, are you excited for the benefit?"

I gave him a look that said, "What do you think?"

His mouth stretched into a wide smile, and he looked handsome like always. Our waitress was making eyes at him but he didn't seem to notice. He seemed to be oblivious to the world around him. I hadn't even seen him with a girlfriend before. If I didn't know he was straight, I might wonder if he was gay. "Come on, it won't be that bad."

"Socializing with snooty people who can only discuss how much money they have? There are a million other things I'd rather be doing." At least I would have a date. He was pretty quiet and didn't say much. But, he might be interesting.

"It's not my cup of tea either but at least there will be free food—and booze."

"Booze is good."

He took another sip of his soda then tapped his knuckles on the counter lightly. His eyes were downcast, and his thoughts seemed to be elsewhere. When he finally gathered his ideas, he spoke. "How about we go together?" His eyes turned to my face and he watched my reaction.

Uh...this was awkward.

Joey continued to watch me, his eyes guarded. But I knew he was hoping for a yes.

"Actually, I already have a date." He'd never asked me something like this before so I wasn't prepared to give the answer.

He stared at me blankly, like he was still waiting for me to respond. Then his eyes fell noticeably. His shoulders relaxed like there was no strength left in his muscles. He looked away, a quizzical expression on his face.

I looked down because I didn't like his reaction.

Then Joey turned his gaze on me, still caught off guard. "A date?"

I understood his skepticism since I never brought a date to anything. I never dated anyone and I never brought anyone around the family. "Yeah. His name is Cato."

"Cato..." He said the name like it was displeasing.

"We've been seeing each other for a while...I thought I'd bring him around."

Now he looked appalled. "You've been seeing someone?" Disbelief was in his voice. "When...how...what?" He completely lost his composure and wasn't the calm and cocky friend I knew.

"We met through mutual friends and...it just happened." I tried to be as vague as possible. I was a terrible liar and I couldn't pull off something complex. The less detail I gave, the easier I'd be able to carry this story.

"How long has this been going on for?" His food was abandoned.

"I don't know...a while." *Stay vague.*

"Oh." He nodded. "Oh..." He nodded again. "I see."

I'd never seen Joey react that way so I wasn't sure what to say.

"Cato..." He said the name again, letting it roll off his tongue.

"Yeah..." *Why was this so awkward right now?*

He ran his fingers through his hair, catching looks as he did it, and then stood up abruptly. "Actually...I have somewhere to be. I'll talk to you later." He wouldn't look at me as he spoke.

"Joey?"

He walked away without turning back.

The waitress brought the tab and left it on the counter.

Joey always insisted on paying for everything, and it was even more odd for him just to storm out like that. He was clearly flustered and uncomfortable by what I said. I wasn't sure what to make of it.

What just happened?

***

I did my hair in an elaborate up do and applied dark eye shadow around my eyes. I wore a maroon gown that reached the floor, and it reminded me of the color of the grapes we used on the vineyard.

Right at six, Cato knocked on the door.

My escort was exactly what I paid for. He was extremely good-looking and got right to the point. He didn't insert fillers into conversations, and he did what he was told.

It was the best investment I ever made.

But he did look familiar. I couldn't quite put my thumb on it. Perhaps I'd seen him on a billboard or in a magazine. With looks like that, he was obviously a model on the side. He had the large muscles of a man who hit the gym often, and he had a dark side to him. I could tell he was dangerous even though I couldn't exactly explain how I knew that.

I opened the door and tried to hide my reaction to him. He wore a three-piece black suit with a gray tie. It fit him to a T and he looked like a million dollar man. His shoulders were outlined in the crisp jacket, and his legs were lean and long. Shiny dress shoes were on his feet. He was every inch of an ideal man. "Hello, Cato." I managed to keep the blush out of my cheeks and greet him as a friend. He was someone I wouldn't mind having a fling with, but Danielle made it clear nothing physical could happen with my escort. It would immediately terminate the arrangement. At the time, I didn't think it would be an issue. But now that I looked at him, I realized just how hard it would be to keep my hands to myself.

"Hello, Katarina. You look lovely this evening."

"Thank you." *He was hot and he had manners. Score.*

"Ready to go?" he asked as he put his hands in his pockets.

I grabbed the tiny clutch that could barely fit anything inside and we walked out together. "Where's your car?"

"Right here." He walked to a black Audi A7 and opened the passenger door for me.

Wow, no wonder why he was so pricey. I got inside then watched him close the door. When he walked around the car, I got a nice view of his ass. *It was very nice.*

Cato drove with one hand and migrated through the city with ease. The radio was on and he didn't make small talk. He kept to himself.

It was relaxing.

I looked out the window and watched the city lights disappear as we entered Connecticut. The benefit was taking place at the vineyard and it would be nice to see the wide-open spaces again.

Cato finally spoke. "Here?"

"Yeah. Follow the roundabout and the valet will take your car."

He nodded then pulled over.

The valet took my hand and helped me out, but Cato came to him and snatched me away quickly. He tucked my arm through his and kept me close. "How do you want me to behave?" he said quietly into my ear.

"I don't understand your meaning."

"Do you want me to be all over you, madly in love, or do you want me to be distant but clearly be your date?"

People wouldn't believe this would last unless we acted like we were in love. "The first one."

"Okay." He escorted me inside until we entered the ballroom. People held glass flutes while they quietly mingled. The women were dressed in their finest gowns, and the men wore designer suits.

I just had to stay for a few hours, mingle, and then Cato and I could hightail it out of there.

"Can I get you a drink?" Cato asked politely.

"Sure."

"Champagne?"

"Yes, please."

"Coming right up." He approached a passing waiter and grabbed two glasses. Then he returned and handed me one.

I immediately downed it then released a satisfied gasp.

He watched me with interest, his blue eyes dark and stunning like the skin of a blue whale. "You either have a drinking problem or you really don't want to be here."

"Both."

He nodded then sipped his glass. "Anything I should know about your family?"

"Just pretend your rich and you'll fit in with everyone else."

"I *am* rich."

"But don't tell them you're an escort."

"I've been doing this for a long time," he said without looking at me. "I have a cover story."

"Don't get caught up in your lies. My parents have a good memory."

"You obviously didn't inherit that."

I turned to him, and my eyebrow arched. "Sorry?" What did he mean by that? At first, I thought Cato was the strong and silent type. Now I got the impression he didn't like me. But why? He hardly knew me.

"Nothing," he said vaguely.

Okay...that was weird.

"Where this guy who's intent on marrying you?" He searched the crowd with one arm around my waist.

"His name is Joey."

"Good to know."

"And I'm not sure." Based on his peculiar behavior he may not even want to see me. "Don't expect to run into him tonight."

"Why not?"

"We had…a weird thing last week." I thought it was odd we hadn't spoken since. Joey usually texted me throughout the week.

"A weird thing?" he asked. "Is that how you describe hook-ups?"

How did he jump to that conclusion? "No…when I told him I had a date he acted weird. That's all."

Cato sipped his glass again and held his silence.

I tugged him along and made introductions to people I worked with. As the inheritor of the wine company, I had to make a good impression to everyone my father was connected with. People were nice, for the most part, but they were also fake. If my family lost everything we had, they wouldn't still call us friends. They would ride in the limo with us, but the second it broke down and we needed a cab, they would bail.

Cato had impeccable manners, and like he was a completely different person, he was charming and funny. He had a quick wit and easily made everyone adore him. He was making such a good impression I wasn't sure if I was paying him enough money.

When we walked away from the crowd, I spoke quietly to him. "Why don't you use that charm on me?"

His happy countenance disappeared the moment there wasn't an audience. "It didn't seem like it worked."

"You haven't tried."

"Actually, I have." He headed to the bar without telling me what he was doing. He ordered a scotch, downed it with a quick swallow, and then slowly made his way over to me.

What was I missing? He was so vague and said all these ominous things. *What was the deal?*

He returned to my side. "Now, where are your parents?"

"Do you have a problem with me?" I blurted.

He lowered his hand from my waist for a moment and regarded me coldly. The look was icy and covered in frost. I didn't even need him to answer the question at that point. "I'm doing my job and I'm doing it well. So, what does it matter? You don't strike me as a kind of woman with deep emotions."

Again, he was subtly insulting me. "If I did something to offend you, I'm sorry."

He looked away and put his arm around my waist. Let's meet the parents."

The subject seemed to be dropped. I couldn't figure out why Cato was being so disgruntled toward me. What did I do to him? But he was right. He was doing what I paid him to do, and he was already causing ripples through the crowd. Now it was too late to back out and switch him with a different escort. I'd have to deal with him and his odd prejudice.

Mom and Dad were talking quietly together. Dad wore an Armani suit, and his slightly gray hair matched the color. His mustache was the same color, and he wore slightly large eyeglasses. Mom was seven years younger than him, and their age difference was obvious. She was good-looking for her age, and she still ran marathons religiously. She was a typical trophy wife, someone my dad married solely for her looks. When they spotted us, Mom's jaw was practically on the floor. Dad did a double take, clearly surprised I brought a man to the benefit.

"There they are," I said quietly to Cato.

"I could tell she was your mom without you pointing it out. You look a lot alike."

"Thanks...I think."

"It was a compliment." He pulled me close to him then approached my parents. "Good evening, sir. It's a pleasure to meet you." Cato shook his hand and introduced himself.

Dad was impressed from the beginning. "I didn't realize my daughter was bringing a date, and such a charming young man."

"She's the charming one, sir." He turned to me and gave me an affectionate look. It seemed genuine to everyone else, but I knew it was just an act. He made it abundantly clear he didn't fancy me.

I gave him a fake smile in return and acted like I adored him.

Then Cato approached my mother and swept her off her feet. "I would have thought you two were sisters."

She blushed and waved his comment away. "I'm much younger than my husband, but it worked out well." She rubbed Dad's shoulder. "He gets more handsome as he ages."

"You guys look really happy," Cato noted. His arm snaked back to my side. "I can only hope I'll have something like that someday." He gave me a particular look, saying a lot without using words.

Man, he was smooth.

My parents watched us intently.

Then Cato made small talk with my parents, keeping up with their aristocratic tones and customs. He fit right in, like he belonged at this benefit. But then I remembered he did this for a living, so he had a lot of practice.

Cato politely excused himself then headed to the bathroom. When he was gone, my parents immediately rounded on me.

"I didn't know you were seeing someone."

"Where did you find him?"

"What about Joey?"

All the questions came out at the same time. I felt like I was in a batting cage and the ball machine wouldn't stop throwing high-speed baseballs at me. "We've been seeing each other for a few weeks and I really care about him. I think this is going to go somewhere."

Mom's eyes shined with joy, but there was also apprehension. She turned to Dad, having a silent conversation with him. I knew they were rooting for Joey, hoping we would settle down together. We'd been friends since we were kids. I wasn't sure why they thought anything would ever happen between us. Men had come and gone from my life and Joey was never one of them.

"Honey, maybe you should at least give Joey a chance," she said gently. "You guys are so perfect together."

I tried not to snap. I knew she meant well. "Mom, no. It'll never happen."

"Even if you don't love him, the marriage is so convenient," Dad reasoned. "He's your best friend and business partner. That was the original reason marriage was practiced."

A loveless marriage was ideal for me. I would never love anyone else for as long as I lived. It wasn't an option for me, and it never will be. I understood why my parents wanted a relationship with Joey to happen. It gave me what I needed.

But I didn't want that. "No."

Mom lowered her voice. "I was always under the impression that..."

"Things change." I didn't want to hear her say it. Even after all these years, it was still too painful. Perhaps repressing my emotions was making me feel worse but I couldn't confront them head-on. I simply wasn't strong enough. "I appreciate your concern but Joey isn't right for me. He and I can still be great business partners as friends. It's what we've always done."

Mom and Dad fell silent, losing the argument.

Fortunately, Cato returned and his arm moved around my waist. "Did I miss anything?"

"No," I said. "Nothing at all."

***

Cato ate with perfect manners and I didn't have to keep an eye on him. He made appropriate conversation with the people joining us at the table, keeping his hand on my thigh as he did so. It was unfortunate we didn't get along personally because he seemed like a wonderful guy when he wasn't sending jabs my way.

I sipped my drink and noticed Cato and I hardly spoke. He spoke to strangers easier than he spoke to me. He even traded phone numbers with a man from my office so they could go golfing sometime. Would anyone think it was odd that Cato and I hardly spoke to each other?

"Having a good night?" I asked.

"The food is good." That was all he said. He didn't even answer my question.

"And the booze?"

"That's even better," he said. "So, did I help you reach your goals?"

"I think so—for the most part."

"Meaning...?"

"My parents still want me to be with Joey. They accept you and even like you, but they find our relationship a little odd."

"Why?"

"I just don't usually date."

That caught his interest and he turned his full attention on me. "Why is that?"

I didn't want to talk about it—especially with a man I hardly knew and who was rude to me most of the time. "I just don't." I took a drink after I spoke, something for me to do so I wouldn't have to look at him.

He backed off. "Maybe they want you to get out a little."

I ignored the jab because he didn't know what he was talking about. If he'd known what I'd been through, he'd shut his mouth and stay quiet.

Fortunately, the auction began and people bid on different bottles of wine, including a very special one that was two hundred years old. That sold for a whopping half a million. I was surprised people thought it was worth that much. At least it was going to charity.

Cato kept his hand on my thigh but remained silent. He and I didn't speak much because there was nothing to talk about. Perhaps he was just a good actor, but I wondered why he could be so pleasant to everyone else but me. Did he not respect me because I paid for his time? That would be hypocritical. I wish it wouldn't bother me.

But it did, for some reason.

After the dinner was over and people began to mingle again, I grabbed another drink and walked around with Cato. I made a few more introductions, and by the end of the night, Cato seemed to have met everyone important.

"That's a lot of names to remember," he said.

"You get use to it," I said vaguely.

Cato remained by my side, being affectionate with me like a man deeply in love.

I sipped my wine and looked around the room when I came upon a face, I knew so well I froze. Joey was watching us together, and he didn't look happy at all. He was ghostly white and bloodless. His expression was blank but his eyes were full of disappointment.

Should I talk to him? What would I say?

"That's Joey, isn't it?" Cato said without looking directly at him. He was talented at talking about someone without making it obvious.

"Yeah."

"Makes sense."

What did that mean?

"Should we talk to him?" he asked. "How do you want to proceed?"

Sometimes he behaved like a robot. "I guess we should. I don't understand why he's being weird."

The corner of his lip upturned in a smile. "You really can't figure it out?"

"Do you know something I don't?" I snapped slightly, getting sick of his little comments coming at the most unsuspecting times.

"All I had to do was look at him and I figured it out." His voice carried his indifference. Offending me didn't bother him in the least.

"Then enlighten me."

He turned to me, coming dangerously close to my face. "When a guy doesn't like seeing you with another guy, it usually means he wants to fuck you."

His crude words didn't surprise me even though he'd never spoken that way before. "Joey doesn't want to fuck me."

He released a sarcastic laugh. "Woman, you are blind."

"Don't call me that."

"You're blind no matter what I call you." He kept his arm around me but the touch felt cold.

I refused to believe that. Joey and I had been friends forever, and if he had feelings for me he would have said something by now. There was no reason to bide his time. "Let's go. And be polite."

"Have I been anything else this evening?" he demanded.

"To me you have."

An annoyed look came into his eyes and he turned away.

Whatever. "Come on."

Cato held me close as we approached Joey.

Joey didn't look at me. His eyes were glued to Cato. He looked him up and down, sizing him up. There wasn't that usual welcoming look on his face. Joey had the ability to make anyone feel welcome no matter how out of place they felt. But now he just stared at Cato like he was a nuisance at the party.

Cato extended his hand. "It's a pleasure to meet you. Katarina has told me so much about you."

Joey took it but he dropped the embrace quickly, like he didn't want to touch him for a moment longer than he had to. "Likewise," he said coldly.

An awkward silence filled the room.

We stared at each other, unsure what to say.

I cleared my throat. "Having a good time?"

"Yeah." He didn't elaborate or try to carry the conversation. It was completely unlike him. He glanced at Cato again before he turned back to me.

There was clearly something on Joey's mind but he wouldn't admit it when Cato was there.

I turned to Cato and tried to be affectionate. "Babe, can you excuse me for a moment?"

"Sure." He walked away, probably glad to be rid of me.

Once he was out of earshot, I turned to Joey. "What's going on, Joe?"

"I don't understand your meaning."

"You've been weird since we had lunch. What's the deal?"

"Deal?" he asked. "Nothing." He put his hands in his pockets and kept looking at different things, the floor, people nearby, anything but me.

"Did I do something to offend you?"

He stared across the crowd like I wasn't there. "He's good-looking. Where did you find him? At a gym?" His voice was full of loathing.

"No. Why do you ask?"

"Because he looks like a jackass meathead."

"You met him for two seconds…"

"I can just tell." Joey never said anything mean about someone else. It was completely out of character. His behavior was so unusual I didn't know what to make of it.

"Seriously, what's your problem?"

"Problem?" He released a fake laugh. It almost sounded maniacal. "I don't have a problem. You're the one with a problem."

I was clearly getting nowhere with Joey. He was obviously too upset to tell me what was really on his mind.

Since I didn't have any magic up my sleeve to pull it out of him, I gave up. "Have a good night."

"You too," he said coldly. "Enjoy pretty boy."

I gave him one final look before I returned to my date.

Cato was leaning against the bar, looking like a model waiting for his picture to be taken. He had the body fit for an athlete and the face a photographer would kill for. "Told you so."

"Told me so what?"

"He's so into you, Katarina. I hardly know the guy and I can tell."

I was starting to wonder if he was right. I couldn't figure out any other cause of his behavior. "I'm ready to go."

He set his drink down quickly, like he'd been waiting for this night to end just as much as I had. "Then let's hit the road."

***

Cato walked me to my door, and I was surprised he even did that. After the way he discreetly insulted me throughout the night, I was surprised he had any desire to make sure I got to my door in one piece.

"Thank you for tonight," I said politely, hoping to kill him with kindness.

"Yeah..." He kept his hands in his pockets and didn't seem interested in looking at me. "Let me know when you need me."

His detachment was getting annoying. His lack of maturity was getting under my skin, and now I wanted to sink my claws into him and rip him apart. "If you hate your job so much, why do you do it?"

"Who said I hated my job?" He turned his blue eyes on me.

"You don't act like you enjoy it much."

"Perhaps it's just the company," he said coldly.

"Seriously, what did I do to you? I'm a pretty nice person."

"That's debatable…"

I pushed him hard and he stumbled into the opposite wall. "I've been nothing but polite to you from the start. When we first met—"

"You don't even remember when we first met."

"Excuse me?"

He shook his head and didn't say anything.

"What am I missing here?"

His blue eyes looked colder than an ice-berg. "You seriously don't remember?"

"Remember you from where?" I demanded. "Maybe if you told me it would come back to me. You do look familiar but I can't place you."

He held up his hand then lowered it. "Forget I said anything."

"No, there's obviously something bothering you."

"And I doubt you give a shit. You only care about your own feelings, not mine or Joey's."

Why was he being dragged into this? "If you hate me so much, maybe you should just quit."

"I don't bail on a client who needs me. And we both know you can't afford to lose me. You've already introduced me to everyone. There's no going back."

"Well, if you aren't going to tell me how you know me and why you despise me, then can you try to be somewhat civil to me?" I put my hands on my hips. "Because I will kick your ass if I have to."

"Kick my ass?" he asked incredulously.

"Hell yeah I'll kick your ass," I snapped. "I know a front guillotine choke, a stable headlock, and a rear mount. You want to try me?"

He came closer to me but was more than an arm's length away. "Those are all military moves."

"Your point?" I hissed.

"How do you know all that?" He suddenly turned serious, no longer angry or cold like before.

"None of your damn business. Now, are you going to stop being a jackass? I can't deal with you, Joey, and my family. So decide."

He regarded me for a long moment before he headed toward the hallway. "I'll try."

"You'll try?" I yelled after him.

He looked at me before he turned the corner. "It's the best I can do."

***

A knock on my door sounded after midnight.

Who the hell would drop by so late? It was unusual. I was on my guard when I approached the door. When I looked through the peephole, I saw someone I didn't expect.

Joey.

What was he doing here?

I opened the door and studied him closely. "Hey...kinda late to drop by."

His hands were in his pockets and his hair was ruffled like he ran his fingers through it too many times. His eyes were slightly red like he was exhausted. He was still wearing his clothes from the benefit, a suit and tie.

When he didn't respond, I spoke again. "Joey?"

He looked at me like he finally noticed me. "Katarina."

I held the door with one hand just in case I needed to slam it in his face. "Can I help you?"

His eyes were practically black. "What happened to never falling in love again? You said you would never have anyone as long as you lived. But then you bring some boy toy around. What the fuck is that, Katarina?"

He never spoke to me like that before. I didn't think he even had it in him. It was clear he was drunk because his inhibitions were far lower than normal. "You've been drinking."

"What does that matter?" he snapped. "These thoughts exist either way. So, what the hell are you doing?"

"My personal life is none of your business, Joey. You should be ashamed of yourself for talking to me this way, for making me feel guilty over something I shouldn't feel bad about. I'm sick of having our parents push us together. They won't stop unless I give them a reason to stop."

"So you start dating some loser?"

"You know nothing about him." I wanted to confess the truth and say he was an escort but I couldn't trust Joey to keep my secret. With his behavior I wasn't sure if I could trust him at all.

"I know he's not right for you. And that's all I need to know."

I knew I should end this conversation before it went somewhere we could never come back from. Joey was obviously upset and he was saying things he would never spit out if he were sober. I would cut him some slack. "Let's talk tomorrow."

"I want to talk now."

"Joey." My voice cut through the air and even made me flinch. "I have a feeling you're going to say something stupid that will ruin the friendship we have. I'm more than happy to talk to you in the morning. But now, you need to leave."

He stared at me but held his silence. It was clear he wanted to burst and scream. But he made the smart move. "Good night, Kat."

"Good night, Joey."

Cato

I was such a dick to her.

I couldn't stop myself. Years had come and gone, and I thought I was over what happened between us. But when I was around her, I remembered how much that morning hurt. What we had was special but she didn't see it that way. She left me in the middle of the night or early in the morning without saying a word to me. I was grateful I even got a note.

There was no justifiable reason why I should be angry with her. What she did to me, I'd done countless times to others. It was biting me in the ass because I deserved it. I didn't believe in Karma but I was starting to.

For just a moment, I thought I was going to tell her how I knew her. I was going to come clean and say it. But something stopped me. The fact I said we already met and she still couldn't figure it out just pissed me off. What if I told her about that night and she *still* didn't remember it?

It would be devastating to my ego.

The fact she was even more beautiful than I remembered irritated me. Why couldn't she be fat and ugly to make it easier on me? She was graceful and intelligent, beautiful beyond description, and she had a no-bullshit attitude that I immediately loved. When she threatened to attack me, I knew she was being sincere. She wasn't a pushover like most girls.

Katarina was a whole new breed.

I needed to let go of that night and just move on. She was my client now, and being an ass to her wouldn't get me anywhere. It would just make us argue and fight, something I'd rather not do.

I didn't like her friend Joey one bit. He eye-fucked the shit out her, not caring who saw or what they thought. Katarina insisted their families were trying to push them together, but I had a feeling Joey had a hand in that. It seemed like the only person who didn't want it to happen was Katarina.

Why wasn't she dating? She said she never did it. Why? It was an odd thing for a gorgeous woman to say. If that was her philosophy, it made sense why she ditched me the night we met. Maybe she was looking for something quick and simple, what I usually wanted.

But on that night, I didn't want that with her. I wanted something more. It was the first time that ever happened to me, and it wounded me she didn't feel the same way. How could I feel something so extraordinary but it completely escaped her notice?

I was feeling worse by the second. I knew I should apologize to her. Instead of being a perfect date and making her evening perfect, I insulted her left and right. I couldn't control my tongue, and rude things came spilling out. My resentment was unfair, especially since I wouldn't tell her what my problem was. I should be a man and apologize.

***

I knocked and waited for an answer.

Katarina opened the door and studied me suspiciously. "How can I help you?"

Just looking at her pissed me off. That soft brown hair felt amazing in my fingertips. I remembered fisting it, gripping it as I slammed into her. Even two years later, the memory came back to me vividly. Her pussy was so tight and my cock loved every second of it. And when she rode me...I was in heaven.

"Cato?"

My thoughts were shattered by her words. If she knew what I was thinking, she would murder me on the spot, probably with those military moves. I focused my gaze on her face and tried to remember why I was there. "I just came by to apologize for my behavior."

She lowered her guard slightly. "Yeah?"

"Yeah. I was very rude to you and I shouldn't have been."

Katarina lowered her arms to her sides. "Well, thank you. I appreciate that."

"Yeah..."

"However, I'd rather know why you dislike me so much." She searched my face for an answer, hoping I would solve the mystery.

Telling her would be stupid. She still wouldn't remember that night, and then I would feel worse. Two people experienced something great but only one person remembered it. It wasn't worth bringing up. "It's my own problem. Let's just forget about it."

"Well, you were pretty hostile…"

"I'd rather just forget about it." I put my hands in my pockets and shifted my weight to one foot.

"But you still don't look at me the same."

"Pardon?" I asked.

"You still aren't nice, charming, or sweet. You do it to everyone else but me."

"Well, I'm not acting right now."

"So, this is who you really are?" she asked. "Sad and irritable?"

The anger started to burn deep inside me. "I just apologized to you. Now you want to pick a fight?"

"I'm not picking a fight. I just think I'm entitled to know why you dislike me so much." Her nostrils flared.

"Maybe because you're a cold-hearted bitch."

She flinched like she'd been stung. "Excuse me?"

"Come on, it's so obvious Joey is in love with you. It's not that you don't notice. It's that you don't care. People are trying to manipulate your love life because you don't know how to love on your own. When something good is right in front of you, you don't even notice. You're going to die alone and no one will be surprised."

Her fury disappeared like a blown out candle. The grimace wasn't on her face, and her nostrils no longer flared. Instead, her eyes watered immediately, like I hit a trigger that made her snap. She blinked her eyes quickly, trying to dispel the moisture but it didn't work.

Fuck, I'm going to hell. "I'm sorry. I didn't mean that. I was just—"

"Go." She held up her hand to silence me. "Just leave me alone. Please." She walked inside her apartment and locked the door.

I stood in the same spot, unsure what to do with myself. Then I heard the sound of her sniff. She was crying on the other side of the door. She must be leaning against it, because when she started to sob I heard every sound.

I fucking hated myself.
Fucking. Hated. Myself.

E. L. Todd

Katarina

Joey didn't contact me for almost a week after the night he stopped by the apartment. Perhaps he forgot about it after he passed out. That might be the best thing for both of us. He was on the verge of saying something he couldn't take back.

I was at home when he texted me.

I'm ready to talk. Can we meet?

So much for forgetting everything. *Sure. When?*

An hour. At our usual place.

I'll be there.

I wasn't sure how this conversation would go. What did he want to say, and more importantly, how would I respond? Ever since I said Cato's name, our relationship had been turned upside down. Just that simple word had completely changed the game. Could we ever change it back?

*****

I was sipping coffee at the diner when he walked inside. He was fifteen minutes late, and I wondered if he did it on purpose. Joey was punctual to the point of boredom.

He slid into the booth across from me, wearing his casual attire once again. He wore a baseball shirt and denim jeans. When he sat down, he rested his elbows on the table and leaned forward. But he didn't look at me. "Thanks for meeting me."

"Sure."

He played with his watch for a moment and then the waitress approached.

"What can I get you, handsome?" she asked.

"A coffee," he answered. "Thank you."

"Coming right up." She gave him a smile before she walked away.

"She's really into you," I noted. "She hits on you every time we come in here."

"I know."

"Then why don't you go for her? She's cute."

He stared at me for a long time. "You know why, Kat. And if you don't, you need to start paying attention."

I sat still but felt my body physically react to his words. Adrenaline was released, and my heart started to pound harder than before. I stared at him with a guarded expression, not wanting to give anything away unless I was absolutely sure.

He sighed then ran both of his hands through his hair. "I'm sorry about my behavior the other night. I wasn't in the right mind and—"

"I know. It's okay."

He pulled back his arms and sat back against the booth. "I'm really struggling with this and I'm sorry I'm taking it out on you."

"Why are you struggling, Joey?" I didn't want there to be any miscommunication between us. It was a dangerous game to make assumptions.

He was quiet for a long time as he gathered his thoughts. "I'm just going to come out and say the truth. I thought you already knew but apparently you don't. I'll spell it out for you."

I tried to remain calm.

"I've always had a thing for you, Kat." He looked me in the eyes as he said it. "You really didn't notice?"

"No…" I was embarrassed to admit it. I was usually observant of the world and those around me. But clearly I'd been wrong.

"I've felt this way for…" He rubbed the back of his neck. "Years. I'm good-looking, I'm wealthy, and we're really good friends. I just assumed maybe, someday, you would feel the same way."

That wasn't possible for me.

"Then Ethan came along and—"

I closed my eyes. Hearing his name still brought me pain. I thought about him every day and would always think of him every day, but it didn't make it easier to hear other people mention him.

Joey seemed to realize his mistake. "I thought I had a chance after he was gone. I never expected you to love me the way you loved him, of course not, but I thought…I would be the next best thing."

I swallowed the lump in my throat, unable to speak.

"And you told me, numerous times, that a relationship was off the table. Not just with me, but with everyone. It was something you couldn't have again. And I completely understood that. I don't blame you for feeling that way. But…I thought we could still have a marriage. Maybe you wouldn't love me the same way, but we could still be life companions. We could still be friends. And maybe one day…you would grow to love me. And we could have kids."

I looked out the window because I couldn't face him.

"But then you brought Cato to the benefit and said you were dating him…for weeks. It went against everything that you said. How could you completely change your mind without telling anyone?"

I wish I could tell him the truth. Then he would understand.

"You were all anyone could talk about that night. No one thought you would bring a man around, especially one who clearly loves you." He stared at me in shock. "It makes more sense for you to marry me then date someone. It's completely out of the ordinary and against your character. How could you do this?"

I continued to look out the window. "I assumed you would be happy for me…"

"I am but...I'm just surprised." He lowered his gaze and stared at his hands. "Why won't you marry me, Kat? We're perfect together. What's stopping you?"

"I don't love you."

"And you love this Cato person?" he asked incredulously. "I see the way he looks at you. But I also see the way you look at him. There's no love there, at all."

"Even so..."

"Kat, just hear me out." He leaned over the table and begged me with his eyes. "You can't love anyone again and I completely understand that. I'm not asking for that. But we could be great together, as friends. We're both invested in our businesses, we have the same hobbies, and we both want kids. A marriage would be perfect for us. I'm okay with you not loving me. But isn't it better than being completely alone? And I could...satisfy you." He watched my face while he spoke. "Come on, Kat. It's exactly what you want."

I finally turned to him. "A loveless marriage would be convenient for me, yes. You understand me better than anyone, you know that I'm obsessed with work, and you know my heart is no longer beating and it certainly will never beat for you. You're a very handsome man, and I'm sure we would have some chemistry in the bedroom. But you're missing a big factor, Joey."

"What?" he asked.

"How can I let this happen when you admitted you loved me?"

He cocked an eyebrow. "I'm not following."

"Maybe I can have a loveless marriage. But can you really marry a woman who will never love you?"

"But you might—"

"I won't," I said firmly. "There's no possibility. So, how can I hurt my friend, someone I love, like that?"

"You won't be hurting me. I understand the situation of the marriage. I'm not expecting you to fall for me. But I hope that you might grow to love me—in a different way."

I stared down at my hands on the table.

"Just think about it, Kat. I don't know what you're doing with Cato but he's not right for you."

"Again, you don't even know him."

"You aren't going to fall in love with him though," he said. "Think about it. You pick me and we get married. Then no one will ever ask you about your love life again. No one will ever question you. Isn't that what you want?"

I couldn't believe he was manipulating me into ruining his life. It would be easy for me, even convenient, but Joey was my friend and I really cared about him. "You know what I think?"

"Hmm?"

"I think you deserve the best, Joey."

He stared at me with bright eyes.

"You deserve a woman who loves you exactly as you are. She'll treasure the ground you walk on, and every day you come home from work, she'll look at you like you're the one person she's been waiting for. Sex won't be just an act. It will be passionate and beautiful. And every day when you see her, you'll wish that time would stop just to enjoy the moment a little longer. I can't give you that, Joey. And it's what you deserve."

He looked out the window and held his silence for a long time. "But you're the only woman I'll ever love this way."

That broke my heart. I wished this wasn't happening. I wished it hadn't come to this. "But I'll never feel the same way."

"And I don't care."

"You will," I said firmly. "One day you will. And I won't sabotage the most beautiful thing in the world. You'll meet the love of your life someday. And you'll thank me."

"How about we get married until that day comes," he said. "If it does."

"No. If I'm in your life, you'll never open your mind."

He sighed in frustration. "Kat, I really—"

"I'll never change my mind about this, Joey. I love you and I'll never hurt you like that. If you didn't love me like that and this was just a proposal for convenience, I would take it in a heartbeat. But under these circumstances, I can't."

He sighed and refused to look at me.

"Joey, this is for the best—for both of us."

"Then what are you doing with Cato?" he asked.

I shrugged. "Fooling around."

"Just fooling around?" he asked incredulously. "Or is this just an act? Did you just bring him to get your parents off your back?"

I wished he didn't know me so well. I wished he couldn't figure me out. "Cato and I have a lot in common.

We're good together. Perhaps he and I can have something convenient someday."

"That's not possible," he said. "The guy is clearly hung up on you."

I tried not to smirk.

He couldn't be more wrong about that.

Cato

"Hand her off to me," Jett said. "If you're struggling this much."

I rested my face in my hands. "I can't."

"Why not?"

"Her entire family has seen me. She can't just show up with a different guy and say she's fallen in love again."

Jett shrugged then drank his beer. "Maybe you should stop being a dick then."

I lowered my hands and looked at him, irritated

"What does it matter that she doesn't remember you?" he asked seriously. "Your pride is that wounded?"

"It's not about pride…"

"Then what?" he demanded.

Should I just tell him? He teased me a lot but he knew when to be serious. "When she and I had our night together…"

"Yeah?"

"I really liked her," I admitted. "And when she took off the following morning without even telling me her name, it hurt." I stared down at the surface of the table because I didn't want to watch his reaction.

Jett didn't say anything for a full minute. "But you were only with her for a few hours."

I shrugged. "It was the first time I ever had a connection with someone. I didn't want it to end. She's the best sex I've ever had and she's so cool. It hurt she didn't feel the same way. Was I the only one who felt it?" I finally looked at him, expecting to see an annoying smirk on his lips or irritation in his eyes.

Jett wasn't doing either of those things. He had a serious look on his face, and he watched me carefully. "Even two years later, it still bothers you?" There was no sarcasm in his voice. It was a serious question.

"Yeah," I admitted. "It does. She's like the one that got away, I guess."

"Wow..." He nodded even though he wasn't agreeing to anything.

"What?"

"I just never expected you to feel that way about someone."

"Neither did I," I admitted.

"Dude, just tell her."

"I considered that," I said darkly.

"And why aren't you going to tell her?"

I shrugged. "If she doesn't remember me, that night obviously meant nothing to her. Me reminding her won't change anything. It wasn't memorable to her. I accept that."

"Do you really?" he asked.

"Yes."

"Then you need to stop making this girl cry."

"I know." I covered my face again. "Man, I feel like shit."

"Apologize."

"I will…"

"You know what I think you should do?"

"Hmm?" I lowered my hands.

"Try to get her to remember without actually telling her."

I cocked an eyebrow, unsure what he meant.

"You know, take her to Times Square for lunch. Buy some Oreos and make her eat one. Take her to your apartment since she's already been there. You get what I'm saying?"

"You think that might trigger it?"

"Yeah," he said. "And see what her reaction is. Maybe she had an accident after that and had temporary amnesia. You don't know what happened. I find it hard to believe that someone could completely forget someone they've already met."

"I do too…"

"But apologize to her for now…and don't fuck it up again."

"I'll try but you know me." I sighed at the end.

"And maybe when you're on better terms, you can start a new relationship. If she's the cool chick you say she is, then she must still be that person."

"Actually, she's really stern and…rigid. She's not playful like she used to be."

"Bring it out of her." He winked at me. "You know you can do it."

I was good at soaking panties.

***

I waited outside her door for her to come home from work. I wore dark jeans that hung low on my hips and a gray t-shirt. I asked Danielle's advice before I came over here, wanting to make sure I looked as attractive as possible. Katarina couldn't be completely immune. She wanted me once before.

She came down the hallway with her purse and a large satchel, which I assumed carried a million documents inside. It looked heavy, like a kettle bell. She snaked her keys out of her purse as she walked, and she didn't notice me until she reached her door.

Katarina immediately adjusted her keys until they pointed at me through her knuckles, making them look like sharp daggers that could scratch my eyes out. Once she realized it was me she dropped her hand.

I was glad that was her reaction. Most women were oblivious to their surroundings. I'm glad Katarina knew how to take care of herself. "I'm sorry if I scared you."

"I'm not scared of anything." She unlocked her door and walked inside.

I stayed outside since she never invited me in.

She set her things on the table, and judging the slight shake of the table when she set down her satchel, it was extremely heavy. "How can I help you?" She wore a pencil skirt and pink blouse. Her curves were outlined and I remembered the way her hips felt in my hands when she bounced on my dick.

I shook the thought away before I got hard. "I want to take you out to dinner."

"Thank you. But, no thank you." She flattened her shirt with her hand then walked back to me. She rested one hand on the door like she was ready to close it.

"I want to apologize for my behavior last week."

"Apology accepted." She started to close the door. "Good night."

I pushed the door back. "Katarina, have dinner with me." Now it wasn't a request. "I admit I was an ass to you and I want to prove that I can be a gentleman. I want us to be friends. Give me another chance."

She straightened and gave me a powerful look. "Our relationship is strictly business. I don't care if you're an ass or not. Just do your job and we won't have any problems."

I knew she wasn't being truthful. "Yes, you do. Let me prove I'm not an ass."

She crossed her arms over her chest.

"Come on. I want to apologize and make up for what I said."

"Cato, it's really unnecessary."

I took a more aggressive approach. "I'm going to bother you endlessly unless you have dinner with me. If not today, then tomorrow. If not then, then the following day. Save yourself some time."

She stared at the floor for a moment before she returned her gaze to me. "Fine."

"Thank you."

She grabbed her purse then walked out.

"What are you in the mood for?" I asked.

"Anything. I'm not picky."

"Italian?"

"Sounds good to me." She walked beside me but kept a few feet between us. We walked down the sidewalk and I had my hands in my pockets. She stared at the shops we passed and didn't make conversation with me. I didn't speak either because I didn't know what to say.

Once we entered the restaurant and took our seats, I stared openly into her face, noting the blue eyes I'd never forgotten. Her face was perfect, her features blending together but standing out at the same time. Her hair had a shiny look to it, like it was softer than the highest quality silk on the planet.

She looked at her menu and ignored my look.

"What are you getting?" I asked.

"Not sure...chicken alfredo looks good."

"That sounds good," I said. "That's what I'll get."

"I'm glad I could help you with your decision," she said as she continued to look at her menu. Then she finally set it down.

I grabbed the wine list. "What do you recommend?"

"Why are you asking me?"

"I assume you're a wine aficionado."

She grabbed the menu and examined it. "It depends on your preference. I prefer white wine over red, myself."

"How about you choose a bottle for the table? I trust your judgment."

She finally gave me a slight smile, no matter how slight it was.

When the waiter came over, I ordered dinner for both of us, and Katarina ordered the wine. When he was gone, we were alone once more. We were seated right next to the window so there was something for us to look at when it became too uncomfortable.

This would be a good time to apologize. "I'm sorry for what I said last time we were together. I won't behave that way anymore. You have my word."

She glanced at the glowing candle on the table before she turned her gaze to me. "I accept your apology."

"I want you to know I've felt like shit this entire week for making you cry." It was the truth.

"Don't feel guilty. The only one responsible for my emotions is me." She gave me a gentle smile before she looked out the window again.

She was so stiff, nothing like she used to be. What happened to her? "So, we're okay?"

"Yes, Cato."

"Thank you for having dinner with me."

"Sure," she said. "It's nice to get out."

She didn't seem like she had much of a nightlife. "I'm sure you do lots of fun stuff with your friends."

"We do," she agreed. "But they both have boyfriends right now so they're usually home on the weekends, not that I care. I'm happy for them."

I tried to think of something else to say. "So, have you talked to Joey?"

She turned her gaze on me, and the candle reflected in her eyes, just like the lights from New Year's. "I did."

"And how did that go?"

"You were right about him." She said it simply and without emotion. "Unfortunately."

"He seems like a nice guy, and he's decent looking. I'm surprised you aren't interested in him especially since you guys are such good friends." I was relieved she wasn't interested in him although I wasn't sure why. I doubted she would ever be interested in me.

"Joey is a great guy. I respect him very much. But...there's nothing there."

I was glad to hear that. "How long have you known each other?"

She shrugged. "I couldn't even tell you. Since we were born, I suppose."

"Maybe that's why," he said. "He was in the friend zone from the beginning."

"Possibly," she said.

"Did you put him down easy?" I asked.

"I did, but I get the impression he doesn't accept it. He seems intent on marrying me, even if the relationship is loveless."

"He must really love you," I noted. "To settle for a woman who will never feel the same way."

"I tried to explain to him that it would be the biggest mistake of his life. Naturally, he didn't believe me."

"Marrying you doesn't seem like a mistake," I blurted.

She turned her hypnotic blue eyes on me. "Joey deserves the best. I know there's someone out there who will love him the way he should be loved. I love him, not in the same way, and I wouldn't take that possibility away from him. If he didn't love me and he was looking for the same type of arrangement, then our conversation would have had a very different outcome. But I wouldn't take away his shot of true love."

Her words got my mind working. She obviously believed in love but she didn't have any interest in it. Why? "Why do you want a loveless marriage?"

She grabbed her wine and took a sip. "I just do. It's convenient and easy. And I'll never love again so a loveless marriage with a partner I respect is ideal for me."

So she loved someone before. Was it a bad breakup? Was it an abusive relationship? The curiosity was killing me. "Why have you given up on love?" I asked bluntly.

"I haven't given up on it," she said immediately. "I just can't love someone."

"Why?" I pressed.

She set down her glass and pressed her lips together. "What's your story, Cato? You're a very good-looking guy. You must have your pick up of the crop."

She changed the subject so that topic must be off limits. It was a shame because I was truly interested. "I don't have much of a story."

"No special woman in your life?"

You're the only one. "No."

"Never?" she asked incredulously.

"Well, there was this one girl...we only had a night together."

"What happened?" she asked.

"She and I had a great time and we really hit it off, at least I thought we did. The next morning I woke up and she was gone. I never knew her name." I watched her face, wondering if that would trigger the memory.

It didn't. "You fell in love with this girl in just one night?"

"No," I said immediately. "But I did feel something. That doesn't happen for me very often. Actually, never."

"And that was the end of the story?"

"For the most part," I said vaguely. "I never really got over what she did to me. But, I've done the same to countless women before I met her. I got a taste of my own medicine, really."

She nodded then took another drink of her wine.

"I haven't done that to a girl since."

"So, you sleep around?" she asked without judgment.

"Yeah, pretty much."

"That seems to be the case with extremely good-looking men."

"You think I'm extremely good-looking?" A smile stretched my face.

She chuckled, for the first time. "Come on, Cato. You look in the mirror every day."

"It just seemed like you were immune to my charms."

"I'm not," she said immediately. "But don't worry. Danielle made it very clear you're off limits and I respect that."

That got my heart racing. "What if I wasn't off limits?"

She was about to take another sip before she spoke. "What's your meaning?"

"Would you want me if I were available?" I was desperate to know this answer. I never had to ask a girl this before. It was always obvious in the way they looked at me that they wanted me. But Katarina was impossible to read.

A slow smile stretched her lips. "What does it matter?"

"It matters to me." I continued to stare her down, silently pressing her for an answer.

"Cato, I would sleep with you in a heartbeat." She said it without embarrassment. "But that's just not possible for us, unfortunately."

I had strict rules I wasn't supposed to break, but I desperately wanted to break them. I already had her once, and I really wanted her again. And this time, she wouldn't forget me. I'd make sure of that. "What if it was?"

She set her glass down as she studied me. "But it's not."

"Rules were meant to be broken, right?" A cocky grin stretched my face.

She mirrored my smile. "Cato, this conversation is going to a dangerous place. I suggest we drop it."

"What if I don't want to drop it?"

She regarded me for a long time, like she was studying me intently. "First, you can't stand me. And now you ask me to dinner and invite me to a purely physical relationship? I don't understand you, Cato."

"I was being a dick before. But I've always been attracted to you."

"Do you regularly sleep with your clients?" she asked.

"Never have before."

"And why am I different?"

"You just are."

She released a faint chuckle that was so quiet I could barely hear it. "You're one of the best looking men I've ever seen. You could have any girl, any time. Why are you wasting your effort on me?"

It was a good question. And I didn't have a good answer. "I guess I want what I can't have."

The waiter interrupted the conversation when he brought our meals. After sprinkling parmesan cheese on our dishes, he walked away. Katarina picked up her fork and began to each slowly, dropping the conversation.

I didn't bring it up again because I knew it would get me nowhere. It would be a bad idea to sleep with her again, but I wanted to capture that night again. I wanted her to remember me. Why it was so important to me, I wasn't sure. But it was. "When will you be needing my services again?"

"Soon," she said. "When my parents finally accept our arrangement, then they'll let this fantasy with Joey be buried."

"What would you get out of marrying him?"

"He has a prominent shipping company, which we use often. A marriage would unite our businesses as well as our families. My parents have been planning it since I was five. It's extremely annoying."

"And you've never been interested in him?"

"Nope."

"I'm surprised he didn't go for you sooner," I said. "Why did he wait until I came into the picture?"

"I was unavailable for years and he finally gave up. But when I was single again, he became hopeful."

It sounded like she had a long-term relationship. Maybe he hurt her so much that she couldn't trust anyone again. Perhaps that was why she was so detached from me on that night. Maybe it really was just a one-night stand to her because that's all she wanted. How could I be mad about that? Just because I expected something more didn't mean I would get it. "How long did your relationship last?"

"Two years," she said simply.

"And why did it end?"

She stared down at her plate and pushed her food around with her fork. "I don't want to talk about it." She dismissed me without emotion.

I didn't press the topic even though I was desperate to know. "For what its worth, not all relationships end in heartache. Perhaps if you gave love another chance you would feel differently." Why did I say that? I was giving her love advice for no reason at all. I knew I was just doing it so she would give me a chance, a real one. But it was still a stupid move to make.

"Please don't tell me how to live my life when you know nothing about me." Her voice wasn't cold, but it was void of emotion.

"Let me get to know you."

She gave me a dark look. "I don't understand you, Cato. You hate me but now you want to be my friend?"

"Leave the past in the past," I said. "I'm really a great guy. Please keep an open mind."

"I can tell you're a nice guy. I've always known that even if other people were the recipient of that and I wasn't."

I ate my food slowly, not really hungry. "Are you saying we can never be friends?"

"Not at all."

"So, you're willing to try?"

"I wouldn't be having dinner with you if I felt otherwise." She took another drink of her wine.

"Good. Because I think we could get along really well."

She gave me another smile. "Is this a genuine offer? Or are you just trying to sleep with me?"

"If I wanted to sleep with you, I would have done it already." *And I already have.*

"Cocky, are we?" she asked with a chuckle.

"Just confident," I said. "When you no longer need my services, we should revisit this conversation."

"Maybe." She shrugged. "Maybe not."

***

"Let's get some ice cream," I said when we left the restaurant.

"Wow, this is really turning into a nice date," she said with a pretty smile.

"What can I say?" I said. "I'm a dreamy guy."

"And…now it went to shit." She laughed while she looked at me.

I nudged her in the side playfully. "You know I'm kidding."

"Actually, I don't think you are. You are a dreamy guy."

"Well, I try…" I gave her a smile then looked away.

"I knew it." She crossed her arms over her chest while she walked.

We reached an ice cream parlor and walked inside.

"What are you getting?" I asked.

"Milkshake," she blurted.

"Is that your favorite or something?"

"Yep," she said. "It's not messy like a sundae and it's delicious."

"Good point," I said. "I'll get one too."

After we ordered, we sat outside and watched the people walk by.

She took a long gulp then sighed. "Man, that's good. I can't remember the last time I had one."

Her body was perfect so I suspected she didn't eat junk often. "It's pretty delicious."

"You look like you've never had a milkshake in your life."

An egotistical smile stretched my face. "Not necessarily. I just work out harder when I have one."

"Do you work out often?"

"Two hours a day, seven days a week."

She cringed. "God, that sounds terrible."

I laughed. "It's my job. What do you do?"

"At midday, I jog around the vineyards. It's a beautiful trail."

I nodded. "You have nice legs. I suspected you were a runner."

"Have you ever seen my legs?" she asked.

Oh, I've seen a lot more than your legs. "You're wearing a skirt now."

"That only shows the area below my knees."

"I have x-ray vision," I said. "I know how you look."

"That must come in handy."

"It does."

She took another sip. "I need to stop. I'm going to drink this whole damn thing."

"You should," I said. "I'm not judging you."

"Because I'm paying you."

I chuckled. "I was a dick to you and you were paying me."

"Touché." She took another sip. "You know, you're pretty cool when you're being nice."

"You're pleasant too." After I spent a few hours with her, the playful side I used to know came out. She was actually fun and laid-back. It seemed to be a trait she didn't share very often. "I like spending time with you."

"Again, because I'm paying you."

"Last time I checked, I was doing this for free."

She nodded in agreement. "True. So, tell me about being an escort."

"There's not much to tell."

"You have to have some stories," she said. "It's such an usual profession. How did it start?"

"When my friends and I graduated college, it just happened. Girls were asking us to pose as their boyfriends then we just started charging money. We all had loans to pay back so that was why we made the decision to start Beautiful Entourage. It was just a temporary gig until we found big boy jobs. But then it took off and we started making more money than we would ever make doing anything else. And here we are, five years later."

"Interesting," she said. "Do you like your job?"

"For the most part. I definitely wouldn't want to do something else. I have a lot of control over what I do, and I do get satisfaction from helping people."

"Helping people?" she asked.

"Yeah," I said. "When I successfully make an ex-boyfriend jealous or I make my client show her family that she's more than capable of bringing home a pretty boy, it makes me happy. The day they no longer need me is what I look forward to most. It means I succeeded. Honestly, I become a friend more than anything else. A lot of people think I'm some mindless prostitute but they have no idea what I really do. One of my clients is an eighty two year old woman in a retirement home. I visit her every week and we play games and I read to her. So, I do more than just pose as a boyfriend."

She stopped sipping her milkshake and turned her full gaze on me. "That impresses me."

"Thank you. It's nice to get some respect once in a while."

"What's this lady like?"

"The one in the retirement home?" I asked.

"Yeah."

"Well, her husband passed away twenty years ago and she doesn't have any kids. She pays me to be her grandson. I spend holidays with her sometimes too. She's very nice, just lonely."

"I didn't realize you guys did other things."

"Yeah, a friend of mine plays checkers with an old man at the park every Sunday. He says it's actually pretty fun. A few months ago I posed as a groomsmen for a guy who didn't have many friends."

"And I bet you slept with a few of the bridesmaids," she teased.

"All three of them, actually," I said honestly.

She chuckled. "It sounds like a dream job."

"Yeah, I like it a lot. Like all jobs, it has its cons."

"Like what?" she asked.

"Psycho ex's that want to kill me, girls that get too clingy and want something more, girls who try to drug me and sleep with me...things like that."

"Girls drug you?" she asked incredulously.

"Unfortunately."

She shook her head in disgust. "That's terrible."

"It's a job hazard and I try not to think about it too much."

"They should serve prison time for that."

I changed the subject because this topic made me upset. "I have one client that has been paying me to pose as her husband for years. That's interesting."

"Her husband?" she asked incredulously. "How does she manage that?"

"I just go with her to family functions and wear a ring."

"But why does she need that kind of service?"

"Her husband passed away years ago and people kept harassing her to move on with someone new. She refuses to remarry or even date someone. This is just a way to give her peace and I understand that."

Katarina turned to me and stared at me intently. Her milkshake was abandoned, and she looked at me with new eyes, like she never really noticed me before.

"What?" *Did I miss something?*

"I didn't know you guys provided services like that..."

"We pretty much do everything," I said. "Anything you can think of, we've probably done it."

She scratched the Styrofoam of her cup and fell into silence. She seemed to be elsewhere, her thoughts unknown.

I wasn't sure what I said to make her so subdued but I obviously said something. "Did I offend you in some way?"

She snapped out of her reverie. "No, I just drifted for a moment there..."

There was obviously something on her mind. I'd give anything to know what it was.

***

I walked her to her door. "I had a good time tonight. Thank you for spending the evening with me."

"Thank you for dinner," she said politely. "And the milkshake I shouldn't have finished."

"Hey, you can afford a few extra calories," I said with a smile.

She smiled slightly but didn't respond.

"I'm really glad we went out. And I'm glad you and I are friends."

"Me too," she said. "Listening to you insult me left and right got old..." There was a teasing note in her voice.

"Yeah...sorry about that."

"I really wish I knew what your problem was." She looked to me for an answer, silently hoping I would finally tell her.

It was best to leave the past where it belonged. She was opening up to me and I didn't want to make it awkward. Hopefully, she would realize it on her own. If not, maybe I could have a second chance anyway. Now that she relaxed around me, it reminded me why I liked her so much to begin with, and not just because she was beautiful. "You remind me of someone I used to know." That was all I said.

"Well, I'm glad your unfair prejudice is over."

"Yeah." I moved in and hugged her without permission.

88

She stiffened at the touch, clearly not expecting it, and then she returned the embrace.

She felt exactly the same as before. She fit into my body perfectly, and her face barely reached my shoulders. The smell of vanilla came into my nose and her soft hair brushed my shoulder. I'd give anything to touch it, to fist it once more.

The hug lasted longer than I expected and I didn't want it to end.

She eventually pulled away. "Good night, Cato."

"Good night, K."

She turned to me. "K?"

That was what she left in the note on my nightstand. I used it now without thinking. "It just slipped out."

She didn't question it. "I'll see you later."

"Okay." I watched her close the door. Once she was gone from my sight, hope burned through me. That playful and fun relationship was back. Maybe we could recapture that night. But this time, I would see her the following morning.

Katarina

My parents invited me for dinner, and of course, they wanted me to take Cato along. They were still shocked I was seeing him and they weren't sure what to make of it. They wanted me to be happy, but at the same time, they wanted me to be with the man they preferred. It would unify our families and only make us stronger.

Being married to Joey wouldn't be terrible. We were great friends and we respected each other. He was extremely handsome, so a physical relationship would probably be satisfying.

But I didn't love him.

When Cato told me he would pose as a husband, that really caught my attention. It would be perfect. I would never have to worry about hurting him because he was only doing it for a paycheck. He would come along and see my family at my beck and call. And everyone would get off my back and stop telling me to move on.

It was perfect.

And Cato wasn't as much of a jackass as I thought. After he apologized and we started to get along, I realized he was someone I genuinely enjoyed being around. He was friendly and charismatic, and of course, he was easy on the eyes. I'd take him on my sheets if there weren't so many complications with it. Meaningless and detached sex was the only type of flings I had.

No love was ever involved. Ever.

It was all I could give.

When I came home from work, I called Cato. "Hey."

"Hey, Milkshake."

I cocked an eyebrow. "Sorry?"

"Milkshake. That's your nickname."

"Do I get any say in this?"

"Nope. So, what can I do for you?"

"I need your services."

"Superman to the rescue," he said dramatically. "What do you need?"

"Dinner with my family tomorrow night."

"I can do that," he said. "Just tell me what you want me to wear."

"I get to decide?" I asked incredulously.

"Yep."

"Wow...money well spent."

He chuckled. "I'd let you dress me up even if you weren't paying me—or undress me."

I smirked even though I wished I wouldn't. "You went from hating me every second to hitting on me every second."

"I like to keep you on your toes."

"Slacks and a collared shirt," I said. "That should be fine."

"What color?"

"That's your discretion," I said.

"Okay, Milkshake."

"Are you seriously going to call me that?" I demanded.

"Yep. It's cute."

"Cute?" I smiled against my will.

"Yeah, you're sweet and delicious."

"How would you know?" I countered.

There was a long pause. "I can just tell."

I rolled my eyes then sighed into the phone. "I'll see you tomorrow."

"You want to go indoor skydiving?"

I flinched at his words. *Did he just ask what I think he asked?* "Sorry, come again?"

"Oh, I could make you come again."

I rolled my eyes. "I never knew you were such a pervert."

"Well, you make it so easy."

"Did you just ask me to go indoor skydiving?"

"Yeah. You've never been?"

"Uh...no." I cocked an eyebrow because it sounded ludicrous.

"Then we have to go. I'll pick you up in half an hour."

"Whoa...hold on, buddy." If he thought I was going to jump off a ledge toward the ground he was smoking something. "I never said I wanted to go."

"Come on. Don't be a pussy, Milkshake."

"I'm not a pussy," I snapped.

"Then let's go. You scared?"

"I'm not scared of anything. I already told you that."

"Then I'll be there in half an hour. Wear jeans."

I opened my mouth to argue. "But—"

Cato hung up.

"Goddammit."

***

Cato arrived at my door in jeans and a t-shirt. His arms were thick and noticeable, and his hair was a little messy, but in a sexy way. "You ready to have a good time?"

I put one hand on my hip. "I never agreed to this."

"Yet, you're wearing jeans and a top like I asked." He gave me a cocky smirk. His blue eyes were bright like the ocean. Sometimes I wanted to swim in its depths.

"I was already wearing this." I lied. I was wearing work attire when we spoke on the phone.

"You're full of it," he said with a laugh. "Now let's go. I promise you'll like it."

"How can you make a promise like that?"

"Because I can." He grabbed my arm and yanked me out the door.

"Why do you want to do this with me anyway?" I demanded.

"You're cool to hang out with. And we're friends, right?"

"Well, of course but..."

"No buts. Let's go."

I growled. "Fine. If I die I'll be pissed."

"If you die, there's a good chance I'll die too. So you can kick my ass when we're in heaven."

"How is that possible?" I asked. "I know I'll be in heaven. But you...not so sure."

He gave me a glare but there was a slight smile on his lips so I knew he was amused, not irritated. "You're brat, you know that?"

"No, I'm sweet and delicious. Remember?"

A serious look came onto his face. "Oh, I remember."

***

After we put on our jumpsuits we approached the ledge and looked down to the bottom of the building.

"Why don't we have parachutes...?" I tried to keep the fear out of my voice. I double-checked my helmet three times to make sure it was on correctly.

Cato wore a red jumpsuit with a blue line down the side. Even in that, he somehow looked hot. Only a truly handsome man could pull that off. A helmet covered his hair and flattened it but he rocked it. "Because it's a vertical wind tunnel. It blows air at the exact speed of a falling object. So the closer you get to the bottom, the more it slows you down."

"Oh..." *So only wind was stopping me from splattering all over the ground?*

He caught my unease. "You'll be fine."

"What if there's a power outage?"

He shrugged. "It's a pretty cool way to go..."

"And I wouldn't mind if I was old. But I'm not."

"Milkshake, it's all good." He patted my shoulder. "Think about it this way. If you die, I die too. So, we'll be together."

"How comforting," I said sarcastically.

"You want me to hold your hand?" he asked seriously.

"Absolutely not."

"Then shut the hell up and let's do this."

"*You* shut the hell up."

He grabbed the front of my jumpsuit then yanked me to his chest. He gave me a quick kiss on the lips, crushing me hard against him. Then he abruptly released me.

I was dizzy because I was so caught off guard.

"Just in case I die." He winked at me then pulled me over the ledge.

"Oh my god..." We fell down fast, reaching the ground floor of the tall building. But we slowed down the closer we came to it. When we stopped and hung in mid-air, the adrenaline evaporated from my body and I could breathe again.

Cato flipped in the air. "Man, that was sick."

I gripped my chest while I hovered like an astronaut. "You didn't even tell me we were going to jump."

He was upside down when he looked at me. "Exactly. It made it more fun."

I tried to smack him but he floated away.

He laughed. "Good luck with that."

I rolled my eyes then enjoyed the freestyle air system. It was really cool after the immediate danger passed. When Cato kissed me, I felt a spark, but it didn't last enough for me to really enjoy it. But I had a feeling he could do wonders with his tongue. "I can't believe you kissed me."

"Hey, I might have died. I wanted the last thing I did on this earth to be kissing a beautiful woman. You can't hold that against me. And don't you dare act like you didn't like it."

"Last time I checked, kissing was a breach of contract."

He smirked, making a dimple form in each cheek. "Don't ask, don't tell, right?"

"No, we aren't two gay officers in the Army."

"Same rules apply."

Our turn was up and we were pulled from the air system. We changed out of our jumpsuits then left the building.

Cato walked beside me with his hands in his pockets. "It was fun, right?"

"Actually, it was."

"See, told you." He nudged me in the side then kept walking.

"It was nice to do something different."

He reached into his pocket and handed me a picture.

I examined it and realized it was a candid picture of us as we fell. I grinned then looked at him. "How did you get this?"

"I paid for it ahead of time then grabbed it on the way out." He pointed at me in the picture. I was smiling with my arms on either side of me. "That girl looks like she's having a good time."

I grinned while I looked at the picture. "It does..." I hadn't had a good time in a while. It was hard for me to experience the world in a joyful way. Some scars run so deep that you can never escape them.

"You better put that in a frame on your nightstand."

"On my nightstand?" I asked. "That's a little weird..."

"Well, it better not go in the bathroom. That's a little weird."

"You don't wan to keep it?" I asked, handing it back to him.

He pushed it back toward me. "No, you keep it."

"Okay." I stuck it in my purse.

"Now what?" he asked.

"What do you mean?"

"Where are we going to eat?"

"You're hungry after almost plummeting to your death?" I asked incredulously.

"You aren't? Almost dying always makes me hungry." He stopped when we reached a pizza parlor. "Pizza sounds good. Let's get some grub."

"Sure," I said with a shrug. "I'll eat—"

"Anything. Yes, I know." He held the door open and allowed me to walk inside first.

I gave him a smile, liking the fact he finished my sentence. "Thanks for getting me out of the house.

Sometimes I forget to live my life." I didn't mean to become so serious. It just came out.

He picked up on the emotion. "My pleasure, Milkshake."

***

Cato appeared at my door wearing dark slacks and a gray collared shirt. His shoulders looked broad and powerful, and his narrow hips looked appetizing in his slacks. If I saw him on the street, he would definitely get my attention. "Checking me out?" A playful grin was on his face.

"No," I lied. "Just making sure you look okay."

"*Okay*?" he asked in mock offense. "Milkshake, we both know I look damn fine."

"Man, you're full of yourself."

"And you wish you were full of *me*."

I turned to him and gave him a playful smack on the arm. "Watch that dirty mouth of yours."

"Did it feel dirty when you kissed it?" he asked as he leaned in.

For just a moment, I wanted to close the gap and press my mouth against his. "I don't know what I felt. I was too afraid of dying to notice anything."

"Yeah...sure."

"I don't remember you being this cocky."

"And I don't remember you playing hard to get."

"What?" I asked. "I've never played hard to get before."

"I guess we remember history very differently."

I didn't know what that meant but I didn't ask. "Let's go before we're late."

"Whoa, hold on." He grabbed my shoulders then positioned me in front of him.

"What?" I asked, feeling anxious to get on the road.

"Now I need to check you out."

I cocked an eyebrow. "You aren't even going to be discreet about it?"

"Why would I be?" He crossed his arms over his chest and looked me up and down. "You look great."

"Thank you."

"Now turn around so I can see your ass."

I smacked him on the arm. "You're unbelievable."

"Let me prove just how accurate that statement really is," he said with a dark voice.

I rolled my eyes. "I'll double your rate if you stop talking."

He grinned then walked out the door. "Good thing I don't care about the money."

***

"More wine, Cato?" Mom asked.

"Yes, please." He moved his glass across the table toward her.

She poured the bottle then set it down. She watched him carefully, like she was taking everything in at once. Both of my parents seemed to like Cato. He was charming and interesting, and of course, he was good-looking. He would give them beautiful grandchildren. But I knew they were still rooting for Joey.

Dad engaged Cato in a conversation about investments when the doorbell rang.

"That must be the Royals," she said as she left the table.

Joey's family was coming tonight. I hoped that didn't include Joey himself. That would be awkward.

Voices trailed from the entryway, and then Mr. And Mrs. Royal joined us, as well as Joey.

But he wasn't alone.

A pretty blonde was on his arm, and they were all over each other.

What the hell was going on?

Everyone greeted each other, and when Joey and I faced each other I wasn't sure what to say. "Nice to see you…" It was lame but I couldn't think of anything else on the spot. I introduced myself to his date. "I'm Katarina. It's nice to meet you."

"Amy," she said as she shook my hand. She smiled and she was extremely bubbly.

I turned to Joey, waiting for an explanation.

Joey gave her a bright smile. "We met at a newsstand." He shrugged. "It's a long, romantic story."

"Well, I'd love to hear it," I said.

"And I'd love to tell it," Joey said. "Another time." He turned to Cato and greeted him with much more warmth than before. They shook hands, and Joey even patted him on the shoulder before he found his seat with Amy.

I sat beside Cato then looked at him.

He looked back at me.

Perhaps we were spending too much time together, but it was becoming easy to read his mind. Even though he didn't react in any noticeable way, I could tell he was just as surprised as I was that Joey brought a date, especially after our last conversation in the diner.

Like before, Cato put his arm around my shoulder and remained affectionate with me. He was a phenomenal actor, and sometimes I forgot I was paying him to behave this way. He charmed everyone at the table, including Joey's parents. I wondered if anyone thought it was odd that both Joey and I brought dates. It was pretty odd to me.

We had dinner and Cato moved his hand to my thigh. He managed to eat with one hand with perfect manners but still act desperately in love with me. A few times he made eyes at me, and he even leaned in and rubbed his nose against mine. I thought he might kiss me, and I admit I was a little disappointed when he didn't.

After dinner, Cato went into the kitchen and helped my mom with the dishes.

He really was worth every penny.

"He's a fine young man," Dad said.

"Thanks," I said. "I like him."

"And that's all that matters, honey." He gave me a sweet smile before he drank his scotch.

We moved into the living room with our beverages. We had small talk, and Joey was more affectionate with Amy than I'd ever seen. They even had a short make out session, which made everyone uncomfortable.

"Thank you for helping me, dear," Mom said to Cato as they joined us.

"Don't mention it," he said. "After cooking a wonderful meal like that, it would be against the law to let you clean."

She brushed off his comment. "Stop."

Mom was clearly smitten.

Cato moved to my side and put his arm around me. "I missed you." He kept his voice low but I was certain everyone could hear him.

"I missed you too."

Then he leaned in and gave me a gentle kiss.

I let the affection ensue, unsure what else to do. But I liked it so it wasn't that big of a deal. His lips were soft and he knew how to use them. They tasted like wine and I wanted more of it. I wanted those lips all over me. I didn't understand why he was kissing me when Danielle made it abundantly clear he wouldn't. But I wasn't complaining.

When the kiss ended, everyone was staring at us. Joey's gaze was intently on us, and the joyous look on his face a moment ago when he was kissing Amy was gone. But then he recovered himself quickly and acted normal. It made me wonder if I ever saw anything to begin with.

After an hour of socializing, people broke off into groups. Mom cornered me on the couch and asked me how the winery was going. She never participated in the business, choosing to do charity work or yoga with her friends. The news she heard was from my father and me.

Cato was talking to my father quietly, and judging all the random names they blurted out, they were talking was about sports.

Mom lowered her voice. "I'm so glad you found someone, dear. We feared this would never happen for you."

"I know, Mom. Thanks." I didn't have the heart to tell her it was an elaborate lie.

"I hope you don't feel guilty. You shouldn't be alone forever."

I didn't feel guilty. But I wasn't doing anything wrong.

"Does that mean Joey is really out of the picture?" she asked sadly.

"Well, he seems pretty busy with his girlfriend anyway..."

"Oh, come on." She gave me that meaningful look I'd grown accustomed to. "He's just trying to make you jealous. I'm sad to see it isn't working."

"No, he isn't," I said. "Joey doesn't play games. And this game wouldn't make any sense at all. I already said I didn't have feelings for him. Therefore, it would be impossible to make me jealous."

"Do you love this man?" She watched me with intent eyes.

"Yes." It was hard to say it out loud, especially when it was completely untrue.

"I'm glad you found happiness. Your father and I were really worried."

"Don't worry about me," I said quietly. "Cato and I are great together."

"Do you think you'll marry him?"

It'd been on my mind lately. "One can only hope."

She eyed Cato for a moment before she turned back to me. "I think it's safe to say he's hoping for the same thing."

If only she knew.

***

After we said good night, we headed home.

Cato was quiet in the driver's seat. He drove with one hand and kept the other in his lap.

I was tired from all the talking and socializing so I looked out the window and leaned my head against the glass.

"So, Joey has a girlfriend?" Cato asked.

"Apparently," I said. "I'm happy for him."

"Don't you think that was a little sudden?" he asked. "He confessed his undying love for you just a few weeks ago and now he's sucking some girl's neck like a vampire?"

"Maybe I hurt him enough to make him move on. I'm happy if that's the case."

He shook his head. "He's up to something."

"What?" I asked.

"I don't know. But he is."

"Well, whatever it is, it's not working."

"Time will tell," he said vaguely.

I watched the trees pass outside the window and noted the skyline of the city in the distance. We were about to enter the bridge. "You're good with my family."

"They are nice people. Easy to get along with."

"Yeah, but you fit in pretty well. My parents are picky when it comes to men."

"Well, I'm not just *any* man." He gave me a playful look before he focused on the road again.

"No, you aren't," I agreed.

"You melted when I kissed you." His comment was random and came out of nowhere.

"No, I didn't. I just played along."

"Bullshit," he said. "You practically melted into a puddle at my feet."

"Again, it's called acting. And you aren't supposed to kiss me anyway."

"I do what I damn well please." He stared straight ahead and glanced in the rearview mirror a few times.

"Do you kiss all your clients?"

"No. Not one."

"Then why do you kiss me?" I asked seriously.

"I think you're hot," he blurted. "Why else would I kiss you?"

I shook my head then looked out the window.

"We both know you liked it but I'll be a gentleman and dropped the subject."

I released a quick laugh. "You're nothing like a gentleman."

"I beg to differ."

We reached the city and he parked along the curb. Then he walked me to my door, keeping his hands in his pockets as he moved. I snaked my keys from my purse and thought about the conversation I wanted to have with Cato. It wasn't light or easy to explain. But he'd had this conversation with other women before. It wasn't that odd.

We stopped in front of my door.

"Why don't you ever invite me inside?" he asked.

"Why would you want to come inside?" I countered.

"To see that picture of us on your nightstand."

"You mean the bathroom?"

He smirked, a teasing glow in his eyes. "No, your nightstand."

"Since when did you get a vote on where I put that picture?"

"Fine, at least the refrigerator."

"Nah, that's tacky."

"And the bathroom isn't?" he asked incredulously.

I chuckled then looked down at my hands. "When I find a place for it, I'll let you know."

"Where is it now?"

"Sitting on my kitchen table."

"Well, that will do. For now." He kept his hands in his pockets but he was standing close to me.

I wasn't sure why I was so nervous to discuss this. Cato was always professional when it came to business. Of all people in the world, he could have this conversation. "There's something I want to ask."

"Yes, I'm into anal."

I rolled my eyes and released a sigh.

He chuckled. "Kidding. What were you going to say?"

"Forget it." Now I didn't have the courage. I turned to the door.

Cato grabbed me and pulled me close to his chest. His face was near mine and a serious look was in his eyes. "I'm sorry. Please tell me." His hands were on my hips, and it somehow felt like he'd touched me this way before, that we'd been intimate somehow. He touched me like he'd done it a hundred times already. "Come on, Katarina."

I stared at his chest for a moment before I found the courage again. "You said you pose as a husband to a client."

"Yeah." He stared at me with confusion in his eyes.

"Could you do the same for me?" Would he think I was weird for asking such a thing? I was already paying him to be my boyfriend so that was weird enough.

His eyes focused on my face and he seemed at a loss of words. "May I ask why?"

"It would make my family happy to see me married off. That's all."

He nodded slowly. "But pretending to be married is a big lie. You're expecting me to commit to this for years."

"I understand it's a lot. I'll pay you a higher rate if that's the issue."

"That's not what I meant," he said quickly. "I thought you hired me so your family would accept the fact you and Joey would never be an item. I think that's been accomplished."

"Well, I want more," I said. "They'll get off my back for good if I settle down."

He rubbed the back of his neck then looked away for a moment. His eyes were dark and distant.

"I don't expect kids if that's what you're worried about." I never wanted to have kids.

"That's not what's on my mind," he said quietly.

"Well, is it something you're willing to do?"

He ran his fingers through his hair, making it messy but in a good way. "I need to know something first."

What?

"Why do you want to pretend to be married? I know it's not because of Joey. There's another reason."

There was another reason.

"Katarina?" he asked. "What is it?"

I held my silence, unable to form the words with my tongue.

"Why won't you tell me?" he asked in a hurt voice. "Do you think I'm going to judge you?"

"No, I just don't want to talk about it." I didn't want to talk about it with Cato, a man I'd just begun to know. Talking about Ethan was hard, and I hated the looks of sympathy people gave me. Every time I discussed it, which hardly happened, I started to cry. "It really doesn't matter anyway."

"But it does matter," he said firmly. "I'm not asking to get into your personal life. I'm asking because it's my job. How do you expect me to help you if you won't tell me what the problem is?"

He was backing me into a corner and I didn't like it. "Cato, do you want the gig or not? I'm not required to tell you anything. So, just accept that."

He finally backed off. "Of course I will. Anything you need, I'm here. But I wish you would trust me and open up to me. I'm your friend, Katarina. Friends talk through their problems."

"And I appreciate that, but there's nothing you can do to help me." *Actually, there was nothing anyone could do.*

He sighed in defeat. "I really hope you change your mind someday."

"Maybe I will...but I don't think I ever will."

He looked at me with pity, the exact look I didn't want to receive. "A beautiful girl like you should never be sad." His voice came out deep and quiet, and his eyes carried his emotion.

I didn't know what to say or how to deal with his sympathy so I looked down.

Cato's fingers moved under my chin and he lifted my face up. He stared into my eyes like he was trying to read me like a book. Then he came close to me and wrapped his arms around me. He held me close like he had no intention of letting go.

It was nice to be held, for no reason at all. It was nice not to feel alone in the world. It was nice to feel like someone cared. I returned his embrace and rested my head against his chest. His heart beat slow and thudded in my ears. I closed my eyes and treasured the affection, unsure why I loved it so much.

Cato

Katarina wanted me to marry her. I would pretend to be her loving husband for years to come. It was a long-term gig and a guarantee of work. The other guys would love the offer because it was easy money. But her request concerned me.

It was one thing to marry a longtime friend for the political advantages even if there was no love involved but to hire someone to be a spouse was a different ballgame. At least if she married Joey she wouldn't be alone. Living a lie like this was a guarantee she never wanted to settle down with anyone.

Why?

I already asked her and she wouldn't confide anything in me. She was a locked chest and I didn't have the key. An ex-boyfriend obviously hurt her, shattered her into unfixable pieces.

I wanted to break his neck.

Whatever he did, he really damaged her. She didn't believe in love and wouldn't even make the effort to give it another chance. Such a loss of faith could only be caused by something unspeakable.

Katarina deserved more than that. She deserved another chance at love. I didn't want to agree to this arrangement because of that reason, but I also wanted to agree so I could show her how different her life could be.

When we hung out, she opened up and let her smile shine through. She laughed and had a good time. Once her guard was down, her happiness and joy was infectious. She was just like the girl I met in Times Square two years ago. The playfulness was her most recognized trait, and she didn't hide it when she was around me. But it took a long time for me to pull it out of her.

Whenever she wasn't thinking about whatever it was that was causing her so much pain, she was a happy person. She let her hair down and ran around like she didn't have a care in the world. When I pushed her into the wind tunnel, she screamed at first but then she embraced the fall. She extended her arms and laughed as she fell to earth. The moment I saw the picture of her I had to buy it. Perhaps it would encourage her to remain this way.

I headed to the winery at lunchtime to see her. Perhaps she and I could get a bite to eat. Whenever I wasn't with her, I was looking for reasons to see her. I'd never gone out of my way to spend time with a girl, but Katarina completely changed the type of guy I was. Sometimes I wondered if I really liked her, or if I just liked her because she was the first woman to reject me. But it didn't really matter.

I arrived at the vineyard then walked inside. The building was classy and elegant, and there were bottles of wine on display. People in black slacks and black collared shirts walked around. There were offices as well as a restaurant inside.

"Can I help you, sir?" a man asked me as I examined my surroundings.

"I'm looking for Katarina."

He nodded. "I see. This way." He led me past the restaurant and down the hallway. The building expanded into different sectors, and we reached a large office and a secretary sat at her desk just outside it.

"Thank you," I said to the man as he walked away.

The young brunette behind the desk looked me up and down, trying to be discreet in her gaze but failing miserably. "Can I help you, sir?"

"I'm here to see Katarina." I loved her name. It was so sexy and it rolled right off the tongue.

"Do you have an appointment?" She opened a binder with a calendar and looked up today's date.

"No. I just wanted to see if she wanted to get lunch."

"She's very busy," she said dismissively.

Her secretary was aggressive but that wasn't necessarily a bad thing. "Could you tell her that her boyfriend wants to take her to lunch?"

"Oh." She nodded her head slowly. "My apologies...I didn't know."

"It's quite alright," I said politely.

"She's with someone right now but I'll let her know you're here."

'Thank you." I put my hands in my pockets and waited.

The secretary made the call. "Your boyfriend is here, Kat." She listened to the other line and nodded. "Right away." She hung up. "Go on in."

Fancy treatment. "Thank you." I opened the door and stepped inside.

Joey was sitting in a large leather chair facing her desk. A yellow notepad sat on his lap and he had one arm propped on the armrest. His fingers rested on his lips. He looked at me when I entered and quietly acknowledged me.

"How are you?" I said politely.

"Well, you?"

"Good. Thank you."

Katarina came around the desk and gave me a confused look. She had no idea why I was here or why I wanted to take her to lunch but she couldn't outright ask me that. She gave me a quick hug and wrapped her arms around my neck.

I took it a step forward and gave her a quick peck on the lips.

She kissed me back then pulled away, giving me that look that said, "Why do you keep kissing me?"

It was hard not to. I'd already kissed her before she hired me, and since I knew how damn good that kiss was I wasn't going to pass it up again. "Hey, baby. Hope you don't mind me stopping by."

"I never mind," she said affectionately.

"I hope I'm not interrupting anything." I glanced at Joey then looked at her again.

"No, work never sleeps here," she said with a sigh. "Joey and I were just going over shipments to Italy."

"Sounds important," I said.

"It's pretty routine."

"I guess that means you're too busy for lunch?" I asked.

She looked at her watch. "You came all the way down here...I can spare a minute."

"It's really not a big deal," I said quickly. Actually, I was deeply disappointed. I made the twenty minute drive to look at her beautiful face and spend time with her. If I was going to get her to open up, I had to give her a reason to.

"No, it's fine," she said immediately. "I just need to grab something for Joey. Take a seat and I'll be right back." She walked out of the office, her hips swaying in the tight skirt she wore. I glanced at her legs and imagined them tight around my waist. My thoughts turned dark and I shook them away.

I took a seat in the other leather chair and rested one ankle on the opposite knee. Joey stared straight ahead and out the window behind her desk. His notepad was untouched. Now that Katarina wasn't around he wasn't nearly as welcoming. "Amy seems nice," I said to break the ice.

He didn't turn my way. "Yeah, she's a sweetheart." His voice was cold.

I already had the impression Amy was just a component in his game, but now I was even more convinced of it. "Why are you trying to convince Katarina you're over her? She doesn't seem to care either way." I wasn't going to pretend I didn't know anything. It made my relationship with Katarina more believable anyway. Why wouldn't she confide Joey's attraction to her boyfriend?

That got his attention. He finally turned in my direction. "I'm not."

Bullshit. "If you say so."

His fingers still rested under his chin. "You know she's only dating you so her family will stop pestering her, right?"

I shrugged. "I don't care. She's a beautiful woman and I get to have her."

Anger flashed in his eyes. Like a shooting star, it passed quickly then disappeared. It happened so fast I wasn't sure if I saw it at all. "You can't give her what she needs. I can."

"But you just said you weren't trying to convince Katarina you were over her…" I caught him in his lie and I smirked without shame. "So Amy is just a ploy?"

He faced forward and didn't say anything.

"I'll keep your secret." I examined Katarina's wall and looked at her degrees.

"You're an asshole, you know that?"

I shrugged. "Yeah, I guess." I didn't rise to anything he said because it pissed him off more.

"I'm the only man who can put her back together," he said. "You're only encouraging her behavior and depression. And you're okay with that?"

"She seems pretty happy with me."

"She's just using you and we both know it," he said darkly.

"And you're lying to Katarina and pretending you don't love her anymore so she'll marry you," I said quietly. "Now look who's the asshole."

"She *should* marry me," he said coldly. "It should have been me to begin with. How she doesn't see that is beyond my understanding. Instead, she went for a cocky pretty boy and got her world ripped apart. She should have chosen me."

That caught my attention. Joey probably knew the reason why Katarina was so closed off and emotionally unavailable. I was desperate to know her secret since she wouldn't tell me. But I would feel like a jackass if I went behind her back and asked Joey about it. But if he told me on his own...that would be a different story. "She made her decision. You should just accept it and move on."

"Easier said than done," he said bitterly. "If she gave me a chance, she would love again. She's just too scared. So she finds you and drags you along like a cat toy on the end of a string. She'll pull you along for a while then cut you loose, just like she always does."

"I'm going to marry her." The words echoed in the office and landed on both of our ears.

He turned to me with frosty eyes. "What did you say?"

"I'm going to marry her." I met his gaze unwaveringly.

He shook his head then turned away again. "No, you aren't."

"I will," I said. "We've already talked about it."

His head snapped in my direction. "You're full of it. She would never remarry—at least for love."

Remarry? So, she used to be married? What happened? Did he leave her for another woman? When did this happen? Maybe she got divorced right before we met and that was why she didn't stick around the following morning. Now my mind was buzzing with more questions. While Joey answered my question, it led to more questions. "She's had enough time to move on. And I'm a very patient man."

He released a light laugh. "Seriously, do you even know her? You talk about her like she's a completely different person."

"Because she's a completely different person with me."

He shook his head. "I assure you, her only interest in a marriage with you is convenience. If you don't want to get your heart dragged through the mud, you should get out while you can."

"She loves me."

"Cut the shit," he said.

"She does," I repeated. "Ask her."

He studied my face, searching for a lie. "That's just not possible. I'm sorry."

"I'm a pretty good-looking guy," I said with a smug look.

He rolled his eyes and fell silent.

I rested my hand on my thigh and wondered what was taking Katarina so long. "Why are you so into her?" I understood her charms and beauty, but this guy was borderline obsessed with her. I didn't like it.

"Because she's the one," he said quietly. "She's been the one since I could remember. I had a real shot with her. We were getting so close. Then Ethan showed up and it all went to shit..."

"Close as friends, probably," I said.

"No. I saw it in her eyes. She was considering me. But then he came into the picture and swept her off her feet. They weren't together very long, two months, before they got married. It had disaster written all over it."

I couldn't imagine Katarina being spontaneous like that. She was so uptight now. Sometimes I caught glimpses of her playful side but it wasn't strong enough to suggest she would marry a man she hardly knew. "She followed her heart. You can't blame her for that. Just because it didn't work out doesn't mean she regrets her decision."

He turned toward me again and narrowed his eyes. He didn't blink while he examined me. "Now I know without a doubt you're full of shit."

I had no idea what he meant by that so I kept my silence. It was the smart thing to do.

"She would never fall in love with another man and not mention Ethan. The fact you don't know what happened is a dead giveaway. This is clearly just a fling and she doesn't trust you."

Fuck, I hoped I didn't screw Katarina over. I wasn't sure how to fix it or what to say. I wasn't even sure what I said to give him the indication I didn't know about Katarina's personal life. "No man wants to hear about his girlfriend's ex-husband." That seemed pretty safe.

"I think they would since he's been dead for five years."

***

After Joey left, Katarina and I walked to the restaurant.

"Is this okay?" she asked. "The closest place is ten minutes away."

"This is excellent." I put my arm around her waist as we headed inside and reached a table. I was in a daze as I moved. I pulled her chair out then sat across from her. I stared out the window and didn't look at the menu. My mind was swarming with thoughts.

Katarina was a widow.

Now everything was making more sense. She refused to love again because her love had already come and gone. Now I felt stupid for assuming it was anything else, like a bad relationship or an abusive boyfriend.

Something like this should change the way I feel. Katarina had already loved and lost, and her experience was so different than mine. I'd never even had a girlfriend.

But it didn't change the way I felt.

While I was sad Katarina lost the man she loved, I thought there was a real possibility she and I could have something. The chemistry was there. I felt it when we slept together, and I know she did too. The friendship was there, and we had formed a companionship that was comfortable and fun. I probably wouldn't feel this way if we hadn't already crossed paths, but we had. She was the only girl who caught my attention, married or not married.

But this would be extremely complicated.

I wanted to talk to her about it but I didn't think now was the best time. We were in a public place and she was at work. Picking at an old wound wasn't smart until we were alone together.

"Cato?" She stared at me with a raised eyebrow. The tone of her voice suggested she had said my name several times before I noticed.

"Hmm?" I stopped thinking about her husband and how he died. Was it an unusual illness? A car crash?

"You okay?" she asked. "You seem...somewhere else."

"Sorry," I said. "I was just thinking about...work."

"And what about it?" she asked.

"We have a meeting coming up." I totally pulled that out of my ass.

"Okay." She looked at her menu. "I thought Joey said something stupid to you."

No, nothing stupid.

"What did you talk about while I was gone?"

Uh... "Amy."

"Is he really into her?"

No. He's still into you. "As far as I can tell."

"Good," she said with a nod. "I'm glad to hear it. Joey deserves a great girl. He's one of the best guys I know."

And he's obsessive and territorial. Since she wanted to marry me, I didn't see the harm in keeping the truth from her. It seemed to make her feel better so I let it go.

"I wasn't expecting you to join me for lunch." She stared at me like she wanted an explanation.

"I missed you." I gave her a smile that she both loved and hated.

She rolled her eyes dramatically. "I'm sure you did."

"A lot, actually." That was the truth. "Want to go paintballing this weekend?"

She stared at me blankly like she hadn't understood me. "What?"

"Paintballing," I said. "You've never been?"

"You can't figure that out based on the look on my face?" she said sarcastically.

I chuckled. "Me and the guys are going. I want you to come."

"I'll pass."

"I'm not taking no for answer."

"I don't even know how to do paintballing."

"You don't *do* paintballing," I said, trying not to laugh. "You *go* paintballing. And you didn't know how to skydive and you did that just fine."

"But that was freefalling," she argued. "Anyone can do that."

"Come on, Milkshake. You're a smart girl. You'll figure it out."

"Thank you for inviting me, Cato. But no thank you."

"Wrong answer," I said. "You're coming even if I have to drag you."

"I'd like to see you try," she said threateningly.

"I'm at least a hundred pounds heavier than you," I argued. "You'll do as I say."

"And I'll stab a pen in your throat and deflate your lungs." She gave me a confident look like she wasn't bluffing.

I smiled. "That's pretty hot."

Both of her eyebrows shot up. "I just threatened to kill you."

"I know...that's hot. If you've got this much of a backbone then you'll be great at paintballing. Other girls will be there too if that's what you're worried about."

"What other girls?" she asked.

"A few of my friends have girlfriends," I explained. "They're attached at the hip. I can't get them to do anything unless they bring them along. Annoying..."

"I don't even know how to play."

"I'll teach you."

She sighed and crossed her arms over her chest.

I leaned forward and lowered my voice. "You want to know what I like about you?"

She watched my face intently. "What?"

"When you get out of your comfort zone, you're a lot of fun to be around. And I like that side of you."

"You can have fun with any other girl."

"That's where you're wrong," I said. "You're the only girl I want to have fun with." I knew I was getting into dangerous territory but that didn't stop me.

She tilted her head to the side. "Are you hitting on me?"

I shrugged. "What if I am?"

"I can never tell if you're joking."

I shrugged again. "I'll tell you after we go paintballing."

"No. Before."

I stared her down and held my silence.

"Cato?"

"Give me your word you'll go paintballing with me and I'll answer your question."

"I don't need to give you my word," she said. "I never lie."

I laughed even though I wish I wouldn't. "You're paying me to be your boyfriend. I'd say you're a big damn liar."

She shook her head. "That's a special circumstance. And I will go paintballing with you."

"No matter what answer I give?"

"Yes."

"Okay," I said. "Yes, I'm hitting on you."

A slow smile stretched her lips. "You're going to get fired, you know that?"

"I can't get fired. I'm a partner in the business."

"You're going to piss off Danielle."

I shrugged. "I piss her off all the time anyway. This is just another thing to add to the pile."

"She looks like she has a good backhand."

I absentmindedly rubbed my cheek. "She does. I know from experience."

"Then maybe you should stop hitting on me."

"I would if you would stop flirting with me."

Katarina gave me an incredulous look. "I don't flirt with you."

"Yes, you do," I said firmly.

"When?" she demanded.

I leaned over the table and grabbed her neck. Then I pulled her lips to mine and gave her a crushing kiss. My hand rested on her neck and relaxed the hold so she could pull away if she wanted to.

But she didn't.

I moved my mouth against hers, tasting her. She reciprocated, releasing a gentle breath inside me.

Then I pulled away to the sound of our lips breaking apart. I gave her a triumphant look.

She looked dazed, like she wasn't sure what just happened. Her lips were slightly parted and her hair was a little messy from where my hand had been. She was speechless, and she grabbed her menu without looking at me.

I rested my elbows on the table and gave her a smug look. "Point proven."

She finally regained her voice but her eyes still looked like they were on a cloud. "Kissing isn't flirting."

"Then what is it?" I asked. "A step past flirting."

"You kissed me. I didn't kiss you."

"Give it time," I said smugly.

"I don't understand you," she said seriously. "You could have any woman you want so why are you trying to go after a client?"

"The heart wants what it wants, baby."

"But I told you I don't date."

"Why not?" I asked.

She looked down at her menu and dismissed me.

Why wouldn't she just tell me? It was nothing to be embarrassed about. "In case you haven't noticed, we've been dating."

"What?" she asked. "Paying for your services doesn't count."

"And what about all the times we hung out without the exchange of funds?" I asked. "There's been quite a few, and now we're going paintballing."

"That's not a date," she argued.

"Yeah, it is."

"Listen to me, Cato." She put her menu down. "I don't date. Period." Anger flashed across her eyes, and I knew this was something she was particularly defensive about.

"Well, you like me and I like you. Let's give it a shot."

"I don't like you," she said with disdain.

"I'll kiss you again if I have to."

"Yes, I'm attracted to you," she admitted. "But that doesn't mean I want anything with you."

"I beg to differ."

She slammed her menu down. "Knock it off, Cato."

"No. I've been patient with you but it's clear you need a push."

"A push?" she asked. "No, I don't."

"You can't hide from the world and refuse human contact," I snapped. "Life is too short to live in misery, and you need to show me that backbone again and look the world in the eye and conquer it. You're stronger than this, Katarina. Put yourself out there and give love another chance."

"You don't know anything about me," she whispered.

"I know you deserve to be happy. Stop shutting yourself down, and let someone in. If you cracked your heart open, just a smidge, you would realize what you're missing out on."

"I don't have a heart to open," she said coldly.

"You do," I said firmly. "I know you do. You really want to live the rest of your life this way, going from meaningless fling to the next meaningless fling? There's a lot more out there and you're missing out on it. Give me a chance, Katarina. You won't regret it."

She stood up. "I'm done with this conversation and your services." She walked off and exited the restaurant.

I sighed as I watched her go. I'd never been in this situation before and I wasn't sure how to handle it. I'd never wanted a woman like this before, let alone a widow. But I wouldn't give up. I wasn't sure why I liked her so much, but I did.

I walked to her office and walked passed her secretary's desk without stopping at her protests. I walked inside then locked the door behind me. Her secretary tried to turn the handle but it wouldn't budge.

Katarina stood at the window and looked across the vineyards her family owned. She didn't turn to face me.

I put my hands in my pockets then came to her side. I looked out the window with her. "It's a beautiful view."

She crossed her arms over her chest. "It can be distracting sometimes."

"I can imagine."

She still wouldn't look at me.

"Katarina—"

"I don't want to talk about this anymore." She held up her hand. "You're wasting your time on me. Trust me."

I watched her face, noting the brightness in her eyes as they reflected the sunlight. "I don't agree with that."

"It's the truth. I don't want to fire you because of all the work we've already done but I will if I have to."

I didn't call her bluff even though I wanted to. I gave her a false sense of security and let her calm down while we looked out the window together. Katarina was good at controlling her emotions. Just a moment ago, she stormed out of the restaurant. But now she was calm and quiet, albeit still upset.

I did something very dangerous but it was the only thing I could think of. I grabbed her hips then scooped her onto her desk. Then I stood between her legs and kissed her.

Katarina's lips were immobile, practically frozen. Her hands were by her sides, not touching me.

I continued to massage her mouth, trying to ignite a spark of life within her. My hands moved to her waist and I pulled her flush against me, feeling the burn of our bodies.

Dark Escort

Then her lips brushed passed mine with delicate tenderness. She tilted her head as she did it, exposing more of her mouth to me.

I took what she offered and kissed her harder. My hand dug into her hair just like before, and I fisted it like I never wanted to stop. I yanked on it gently and pulled her head back, exposing her mouth and throat for me to enjoy.

Her hands moved up my chest and she found the buttons of my shirt. She unbuttoned each one then felt my naked skin. Her fingers moved over the grooves of my abs and my chest. Then they moved to my shoulders and squeezed.

I pulled her skirt up and felt her smooth legs. I loved how toned they were. I wanted to kiss every inch of her and taste the familiar sweetness at the apex of her thighs. My lips left her mouth and I trailed kisses down her jaw to her neck. I ravished her and listened to her breathed hard while I did all the things I already knew she liked. My hands moved to her breasts and I groped them outside her shirt, remembering their perkiness and roundness. A quiet moan escaped her throat, and I loved the way it sounded. Everything was the same as that night. Nothing had changed despite the passage of time.

I picked her up then carried her to the couch against the wall. I lay her down and moved over her. Her legs automatically wrapped around my waist and she dug her fingers into my hair. My hard-on was pressed against her, and I knew she could feel it through my jeans. I rubbed it against her clitoris slightly through her underwear, giving her some enjoyable friction.

Fifteen minutes passed and we were hot and heavy the entire time. My hand explored her body through her clothes, not wanting to rush into something we weren't ready for. I wanted to sleep with her, but I wanted it to be under different conditions than last time.

I wanted her to still be around the next day.

I ended the kiss then pressed my face close to hers. I looked into her eyes, seeing my desire reflected back at me. "Let's not pretend there's nothing here. I'm tired of doing that. We're going to give this a chance and see where it goes. That's not a request." I rose from the couch then adjusted my clothes. I buttoned up my shirt then fixed my hair.

I loved kissing her but I did it to prove a point. She wanted me the way I wanted her. And it wasn't just physical. There was a connection between us. I felt it two years ago and I'm pretty sure she felt it now.

"I'll see you on Saturday."

She sat up then pulled down her skirt. "What's Saturday?"

"Paintballing."

Katarina

My relationship with Cato was confusing.

When I first hired him, he was rude to me, making jabs whenever possible. When he insulted me, I never really understood why. And he refused to tell me why he disliked me so much.

Then he completely changed.

We became friends and did activities together.

Then he started kissing me in front of my family.

Then he started kissing me whenever he felt like it.

And now I was kissing him back.

My emotions confused me because I hadn't felt this way in many years. Cato was extremely handsome and easy on the eyes. I was attracted to him in a physical way, wanting a night of meaningless passion. But I also wanted something more.

And that made me feel guilty.

Ethan and I had a short time together, but he was the man I married. I missed him every day, and even though five years had gone by it didn't change the way I felt. Sometimes I thought he would walk through the door after work and give me a kiss on the cheek. Sometimes I thought I heard his voice even though it was just my imagination.

After he passed away, I knew I would never marry again. I knew I wouldn't even date again. Sometimes people could love more than once but I didn't think that was possible for me. I had my shot and then it came and went. While I had physical needs that needed to be met, I kept my heart unencumbered.

But now Cato was making me doubt all of that.

I didn't know what to do. When he kissed me, I couldn't stop. When he moved his hands across my body I didn't want him to pull away. Even though his cocky smile was annoying and irritating, I found myself thinking about it throughout the day.

What did that mean?

Was it possible that I was starting to have feelings...for another man?

I didn't know what to make of it. Guilt and shame weighed on my shoulders, and I felt like a terrible person. Ethan told me he wanted me to move on if something ever happened to him but I couldn't picture myself actually doing it.

Until now.

***

I knocked on the door with the tray of fruit in my hands.

My mother-in-law, Cindy, opened the door. She had the same blue eyes Ethan had, and it was nice to see them and remember the way he used to look at me. She gave me a big smile and greeted me like I was her own daughter— like always. "So glad you're here. Come in." She ushered me over the doorstep.

"I brought fruit," I said.

"Thank you, dear. Everyone loves fruit." She put her arm around me and walked me to the kitchen table.

Jim was reading the paper while he sat. A cup of coffee was in front of him.

"Honey, Kat is here," Cindy said.

When he turned to me, a genuine grin stretched on his face. "Hey, beautiful." He stood up and hugged me.

"Hey, Jim." I returned the embrace. "How's the hardware store?"

"Same as always," he said. "No complaints."

Ethan's brother hugged me next. "Hey, sis."

"Hey, Gabe." He looked a lot like his brother so it was nice to feel connected to Ethan even though he wasn't around anymore.

"Fruit?" He made a disgusted face. "That's too healthy for us and you know it." There was a teasing note to his voice.

"I need to keep you guys in line." I set it on the table and took a seat.

Cindy put the plates down and we ate lunch together.

"How are the grapes?" Jim asked.

"Ripe," I said. "We're having a good harvest this year. We changed the soil this planting season and it's made all the difference in the world."

"That's great," Cindy said.

"Are you drunk at work a lot?" Gabe asked.

"What?" I asked. "What kind of question is that?"

"Well, aren't you sampling wine all the time?" he asked seriously.

"No," I said with a laugh. "Well, only sometimes..."

"I wish I could be drunk at work." Gabe was a few years younger than Ethan, and I knew he missed him as much as I did.

"We went to Coney Island last weekend," Cindy said. "We had a lot of fun."

"I ate three hotdogs because they were so good," Jim said.

"Wow," I said, genuinely impressed. "But that has heartburn written all over it."

"Tums," Jim said with a wink.

We had small talk about the weather and the high volume of tourists in the city. They repainted the inside of their house and it looked great. Jim told me he did the work himself, and it could pass as professional work. They asked about my family and the wine business.

"So, Kat...are you seeing anyone?" Cindy asked.

She asked me this question a few times over the past two years. My answer was always the same. "No." I looked at my food as I said it.

Cindy exchanged glances with Jim, and I caught the look in my peripheral vision.

I decided to change the subject before it became too awkward. "You guys should visit Myrtle Beach sometime. It's really beautiful and the waves are always good enough for surfing."

Cindy abandoned her food and rested her elbows on the table. "Honey, we all know you loved Ethan with everything you had. You still miss him, and of course we miss him too. But...you've waited long enough. It's time to move on."

They'd never said anything like that to me before and I wasn't sure how to respond.

Gabe nodded. "My brother wouldn't want you to be alone forever, Kat. He would want you to be happy."

"And you aren't happy," Jim said.

I stared at my food because I wasn't sure whom to look at.

"Don't feel guilty," Cindy said. "Appreciate the time you had together and never forget him, but don't stop living your life because of it. You're still our daughter no matter what. But find a man to introduce us to."

I felt cornered. All eyes were on me. "I'll think about it."

"Will you *really* think about it?" Cindy asked. "Or are you just saying that so we'll drop the subject?"

Ethan's mom knew me better than my own mom. "The second one."

She scooted her chair close to me then rubbed my back. "I know it's hard. I do. But you really need to get out there again. We want grandkids." She gave me a smile and patted me on the back.

"It's just...hard for me to imagine being with anyone else."

"I know," she said sympathetically. "I really do. We all do. But that's never going to happen if you don't at least have an open mind about it. Go on a few dates and experiment. You're too young not to give love another shot."

I nodded. "Okay, I'll think about it—for real this time."

Cindy smiled, and the look reached her eyes. "Good. That's what I wanted to hear."

***

Cato was leaning against the door when I opened it. "You ready for this?" His arms were across his chest, and they bulged with muscle.

"I don't know," I said. "I've never played."

He looked over my shoulder into my apartment. "Are you ever going to invite me inside?"

"Not if you're rude about it."

"Well, you aren't leaving me a choice." He pushed past me and entered the apartment. He looked around then faced me. "Where is it?"

"What?"

"The picture of us. It better not be in the bathroom."

I smiled at his words. "Coffee table."

He walked into the living room and sat on the couch. He grabbed the picture frame and examined it. "It looks good here," he said with a nod. "I'm glad it didn't get stuck in the bathroom."

I chuckled as I sat beside him. "It was a close call…"

There were other pictures on the table, some of me and my friends at the beach, and a few of Ethan and I. I refused to take them down just because he was gone. We had a lot of happy memories I would never forget. Cato examined them but didn't comment.

He turned to me with his arms resting on his thighs. He looked me up and down. "I sincerely hope you aren't wearing that."

I looked down at my white blouse and skinny jeans. "What's wrong with it?"

"You want it to get covered in paint?"

"No…"

He sighed. "Wear something you don't mind getting ruined."

"Well, a heads up would have been nice."

"I assumed you would figure out paint was involved since it's called *paintballing*." He rolled his eyes.

"Don't be a douche."

"A douche?" A laugh escaped his lips. "I've been called a lot of things but never that."

"First time for everything, right?" I stood up to head to my room.

Cato snatched me and pulled me into his lap. "So, still thinking about that last kiss we had?" A cocky grin was on his face and he pulled me close to him, wrapping his thick arms around me so I couldn't escape.

"We kissed?"

Both of his eyebrows shot up. "You don't remember?" Panic came into his eyes.

A large smile broke out on my face. "Kidding."

He growled at me then gave me a hard kiss. "You're lucky you're cute."

I returned the embrace before I untangled myself from his grasp.

He was still leaning forward, like he had no intention of letting me go.

"There's something I want to tell you. I don't like to talk about it but you should know since...you want this to go somewhere."

His eyes turned serious as he examined my face. "I already know, Katarina."

My eyes narrowed because I didn't know what he was talking about. What did he think he knew?

"Joey told me. I'm sorry."

My heart beat fast in my chest. Adrenaline spiked in my blood. He knew about Ethan and I had no idea. It caught me off guard that he already knew the truth but I guess it made it easier.

"I'm sorry that happened to you," he said sincerely. "It must have been hard."

"Yeah..." I couldn't think of a better response.

He watched my face but kept his arms around me.

"I've been alone for the past five years," I explained. "I have physical relationships with men but nothing beyond that. He told me he wanted me to move on...but I just haven't wanted to."

"I think you should," he said. "Five years is a long time, Katarina."

"I know it is. And I know it would make him happy. He wouldn't want me to be alone for the rest of my life."

"Then give it a shot."

"It's still hard to do…"

"Take it slow," he said. "There's no rush."

"But…doesn't it bother you I've already been married?"

"No." He shook his head. "Why would it?"

"Well…I don't think anyone's ideal relationship is with a widow." Was I missing something here? No one dreamed of a spouse that had already been married, especially since we were so young. I met Ethan at a very young age but that didn't stop me from marrying him.

"No, I guess not," he said. "But I've been around a lot. I've slept with more girls than I can count, and I've never wanted to be in a relationship with one person before. But with you…I do. The fact you were once married doesn't bother me. And I think it's been enough time since he passed away that it's appropriate for you to move on."

Cato was one of the most handsome men I've ever seen, and the fact he wanted to be with me was beyond my understanding. "I'm a widowed workaholic. What do you see in me?"

"I see a cool ass chick." He gave me that smirk I'd grown fond of.

It was hard not to melt. Cato lowered my defenses and made me soften. "Okay…but I can't promise anything."

"I'm not asking for promises."

"I just…need to take this slow."

"Works for me." A dimple formed in each cheek.

"I've been with other men because I have needs but I've never—"

He covered my mouth with his hand. "Stop explaining yourself. You talk too much."

My eyes widened in offense.

He kept his hand over my mouth and chuckled. "Much better."

I yanked his arm down. "Jerk."

"But I'm hot so I can get away with it."

"Not *that* hot." I stood up to head to my room.

He smacked my ass playfully. "Not put some real clothes on."

***

We drove to a paintball range on private land in Connecticut. Cato pulled his car over to the side of the road then we got out and opened the trunk. Guns and shields were in the back, as well as the gear.

He grabbed a few things and started to put them on me.

"I have to wear this?" I asked.

"You look stupid but you'll be grateful you wore it." He put the goggles over my eyes then handed me the gun.

I stared at it, surprised how heavy it was. "I'm supposed to shoot people with this?"

"No, you're supposed to throw it at them." He slammed the trunk shut and locked it.

"You're really sarcastic, you know that?"

"And you're damn fine." He tore my mask off and gave me a quick kiss. "Now shut up and let's go."

"Why don't you shut up for once?"

He wiggled his eyebrows at me. "You know exactly how to do that, Milkshake."

I smacked him in the arm playfully.

We reached the entrance area and it was covered in dirt. The area had different trees and buildings for cover. It was an extensive course, easy to get lost in. People were already there, standing near an ice chest as they drank their beers and water.

"Hey, assholes. This is Katarina." He put his arm around me. "But call her Kat. Only I call her Katarina." He turned to me and wiggled his eyebrows again.

I rolled my eyes dramatically.

"I'm Rhett." A good-looking brunette shook my hand. "And this is my lady, Aspen."

She and I shook hands.

He introduced me to the rest of his friends. Every one of the guys was too good-looking to be real.

"They work with you and Beautiful Entourage, don't they?" I asked.

"How did you know?"

"Because they are all hot," I blurted.

He narrowed his eyes at me. "Don't check out my friends. I'll cut off their arms so you won't be tempted to look."

I nudged him in the side. "Are you actually jealous? I didn't think someone so full of themselves could be threatened by anything."

He nudged me back. "With you I am. I don't like to share."

"Hey, sweetheart." The man Cato introduced as River stepped forward. "Ever wondered what it's like to be with a real man?"

Cato held up his gun. "I will shoot you right in the face if you touch her."

River held up his hands and chuckled. "Chill, dude. I'd just thought Kat would like an upgrade."

"More like a downgrade," he said. "Because your dick is smaller than mine."

"Why are you checking out my dick?" River countered.

I tried not to laugh. "Yeah, Cato. What's that about?"

"Don't you gain up on me." Cato shouldered his gun then pulled down his mask. "Are we going to do this or what?"

"What are the teams?" Troy asked. "Harper is on my side." He pulled a blonde into his hip.

"I got Katarina," Cato said immediately. "She's never played before so if anyone takes advantage of her I'll kill him." He said it with complete seriousness.

Troy broke up the teams, and there were four on each side.

"Grace period of one minute." Troy set the timer on the building. It was a large clock and it started to count down to zero.

"Let's go, baby." Cato pulled me to the right and I followed him. I carried my gun, feeling awkward as I did it.

We reached a tree that had a small building at the top. The only way to get to it was to climb.

"Here we go." He grabbed the trunk and started to climb. When he reached the top he looked down. "Do you know how to climb?"

I rolled my eyes. "Yes, I know how to climb."

"Then get that fine ass up here."

I climbed to the top then joined him in the small shack. Cato picked up his gun then positioned it on the open windowsill. He took a knee and focused his gun. "We'll pick them off like flies. Put your gun next to mine. This will be good target practice for you."

"Isn't this cheating?"

"No. It's not my fault they're stupid." He stationed the gun for me then explained how to shoot it. Then he turned to me, a serious look in his eyes. "Okay, now let me explain something carefully. You're going to have the strong urge to kiss me. As much as I would enjoy that, you can't take off your mask, even for a second. If someone accidentally shoots you in the eye...it could be bad. You understand me?"

"I'll try to control myself," I said sarcastically.

"Okay. Good." He turned back to the windowsill. "Alright, when someone runs by you're going to aim and fire."

"But what if I hurt them?" I said immediately.

"It's just a paintball. It might hurt a little but they'll be fine."

I held my gun at the ready.

Aspen jogged by with Rhett behind her.

"Shoot her, baby."

"Are you crazy?" I said immediately. "I'm not shooting her. She's really nice."

He sighed. "When it comes to war, it doesn't matter how nice the enemy is."

His words made me uncomfortable, and I knew exactly why. I tried not to think about it.

"Shoot Rhett. He's a guy. He can handle it."

I held the gun and aimed. I wanted to pull the trigger but I couldn't. "I can't do it..."

"Why not?" He demanded.

"I just can't."

"Fine." He aimed his gun and fired.

Rhett immediately staggered back then fell down for cover.

Everything played in slow motion for me. I saw the way Rhett was hit, the way he touched his side as he felt the paintball smack hard into his skin, and then the way he hit the ground as he tried to crawl to safety.

My heart slammed hard in my chest and I felt sick. I started to sweat and feel faint. If I didn't get out of the situation I would pass out. I fell back onto the floor then scooted back, trying to get space. "Stop! Don't shoot. Stop."

Cato turned to me with confusion in his eyes. He left the gun at the windowsill then rushed to me. "What's wrong? He's not hurt!"

I raised my hand. "Don't come any closer." I pulled my knees to my chest and hugged them. I breathed hard and tried to calm down.

Cato did as I asked and didn't come any closer. He just watched me. "It's just a game, baby. No one gets hurt. It's all just for fun."

I continued to breathe hard and concentrated on a crack in the floor. "I'm sorry...I just didn't realize it would be like this...people shooting at each other."

"And what's the big deal if it is?" he asked. "You'd have a lot of fun if you just tried. I can shoot myself and show you—"

"Don't." I looked at him and commanded him with my eyes.

"Okay, I won't," Cato said quickly. "But talk to me. Why are you freaking out right now?"

I didn't hesitate to tell him. "Ethan was a sergeant in the army. He was killed in combat."

Cato's eyes fell then he dropped his face into his hands. "Fuck...I didn't know."

"It's okay," I whispered. "I didn't know this is how it would be. I've seen violent TV shows with guns and it's never bothered me but...watching it happen in real life just freaked me out." I continued to keep my knees to my chest and that seemed to calm my anxiety.

Cato leaned against the opposite wall and lowered his hands. The battle went on around us, people were laughing and shooting at each other. It seemed distant now that we weren't apart of it. "I feel like an insensitive jerk. I never would have brought you here if you told me that."

"I know, Cato. I probably would have come anyway. I didn't realize how I would feel until it actually happened."

"We can camp out in here until it's over."

"You should keep playing. I'll be fine."

He gave me an incredulous look. "You're really dense sometimes, Milkshake. I'm not going to leave you here by yourself. I'd rather be with you than anywhere else anyway."

The words touched me.

"Now get over here." He patted his chest.

I moved between his legs then rested my back into his chest. He wrapped his arms around me then placed a gentle kiss on my neck. I relaxed and didn't feel scared anymore. I didn't want to participate in the battle but the sound of the action didn't get under my skin.

"Your husband sounded admirable."

"He was."

"You don't strike me as a military type of woman."

"Oh, I'm not," I said immediately. "I never liked the fact he was in the military. Hated it, actually. But he loved it."

"How did you guys meet?"

"I was in New York and he was on leave. We ran into each other at a bar. One thing led to another, and within two weeks we were saying the L word. And then a month later, he proposed. Everyone said it was too soon and we were rushing things but I didn't care. Our relationship only lasted a year. But it was the best year of my life." I'd had plenty of time to come to terms with his death. When I reminisced on our memories it didn't bring me pain. I missed him and always would but I accepted reality, that he was in the past.

"You guys sounded like a bunch of love struck teenagers," he said with a laugh.

"That's a perfect description, actually. We were really young. But I don't have any regrets."

"You shouldn't." He kissed my neck again.

"I shouldn't talk about him..." I realized my mistake. "I'm sorry. I don't mean to make you uncomfortable."

"You didn't," he said. "It doesn't bother me when you talk about him."

"It doesn't?" I asked in surprise.

"Not at all. He was a big part of your life."

"I wouldn't want to hear about one of your ex-girlfriends."

"It's not the same thing," he said quietly. "You've gotten to know me pretty well, so you've figured out I'm not much of a liar. I will tell you exactly what I think and when I'm thinking it."

I laughed. "That's absolutely true."

"So, don't worry about it. I asked about him anyway."

I held his hands as they rested over my stomach. "I was always hesitant to have another relationship because I assumed I would have to bury Ethan in the past and never think about him. I never realized he could still be part of my life."

"I'm glad you realized you were wrong." He kissed my forehead, and his lips burned as they touched my skin.

The last guy to have done that was Ethan, but it didn't bother me that it was with someone new. For the first time, I was glad Cato was in my life. We crossed paths in the strangest way and we were thrown together like our worlds were meant to crash together. It could be the beginning of something great.

And I had a feeling it was.

***

Cato spared me the embarrassment of explaining why we didn't participate in the game. He claimed he had a stomachache and needed to get home. Of course, the guys teased him mercilessly and called him a big pussy but Cato didn't seem to mind.

He took me back to my place then walked inside with me. "Next time we hang out with my friends, it'll be a lot better. I promise."

"It's okay," I said. "It wasn't your fault."

He walked to my refrigerator and opened it. "Got any beer?"

"So, you choose to have manners when you're paid to have them?" I noted.

"Yep." He kept looking. "So...I'm not seeing any beer."

"Because I don't have any. I only have wine."

He closed the refrigerator and cringed. "Well, that needs to change. This isn't a hospitalable environment."

"Then bring your own beer, asshole." I sat on the couch and put my feet up.

He chuckled then sat beside me. "I like it when you call me that."

I turned to him in surprise. "Then you obviously don't know what the word means..."

"I do," he said. "But I like it because it's really obvious you don't mean it." He nudged me in the side.

"Maybe I don't...but don't give me a reason to start meaning it."

"I'll try...but I doubt it'll happen."

I shook my head and fought the slight rise of the corner of my lips. "Won't your friends be upset that you're dating a client?"

"Yep. They'll beat me down when you aren't around. They're jerks, but they do have manners when the ladies are near."

"I didn't get that impression," I said with a laugh.

"Well, they do. They are good guys—when they want to be."

"You're a good guy when you want to be."

He shrugged. "You caught me." He grabbed the remote off the table and turned on the TV. "What are we watching?"

"*The Bachelor.*"

He gave me the most terrified expression I've ever seen.

"Kidding."

He released the air he was holding in his lungs. "Don't ever joke with me like that again."

"I actually prefer *The Bachelorette.*"

"Don't even joke about that."

I laughed. "What? It's a good show."

"Watch whatever you want to watch, but not when a man is in the house."

"A man?" I asked. "Don't talk about yourself like you're super macho."

"I'm the most macho guy on the planet."

"You know what?" I snatched the remote then turned the show on. "We're watching it."

"No!" He covered his face like he was in agony. "I'm going to combust into a ball of fire if you make me watch this."

"No, you won't. Give it a chance."

"Milkshake, you're lucky you're hot."

I chuckled. "Shut up and be a man."

"Then I'd better leave and go cut down a tree or something."

"Shh!" I cupped his cheeks and gave him a kiss. "There. Now be quiet."

He gave a wide smile. "I can do that."

We sat back and watched the show. Cato seemed bored because he kept adjusting his position on the couch. But for the last few minutes of the show, he was leaning forward slightly, like he was on the edge of his seat. Then it ended before the bachelorette could make a decision on whom she wanted to date. "What?" he demanded. "It just ends?"

"Until the next episode."

"She better not pick that blonde guy. He's a douche."

I chuckled. "Sounds like you were interested."

"No," he said immediately. "I just thought a pretty and smart girl like her shouldn't end up with the loser."

"And why do you care?" I pressed.

"I don't," I said immediately.

"Someone's a big chick flick loving girl."

"Am not."

I leaned toward him and gave him my best smile. "I think so."

He watched me then began to cave. "Okay, it's not that bad..."

"I told you."

"I suppose..."

"Now what would you like to watch?" I handed him the remote.

"Really?" he asked in surprise.

"Yeah. We can trade off."

He held up the remote and examined it. "I have so much power..."

I leaned my head on his shoulder then hooked my arm through his. "Pick something."

He put on *South Park*. "Is this okay?"

"I like this show."

"You do?" he asked in surprise.

"Yeah."

"Wow, you're the coolest chick ever."

"Even though I watch *The Bachelorette*?" I questioned.

"Well, that show isn't that bad," I said. "And yes, you're the coolest chick ever."

***

I was signing documents when Cato came into my mind. He wasn't my boyfriend but he was a guy I was sorta...dating...and that didn't bother me like I thought it would. Guilt didn't well up inside me, and I didn't feel like I was doing anything wrong.

But dating a nice guy was nothing like loving one. I feared that would never happen for me. After you loved and lost, it was really difficult to feel that again. Cato didn't seem like he expected anything from me, but I wondered if he would settle for my companionship and my general appreciation for him. Or would that be wrong to let him have just a part of me rather the entire thing?

I wasn't sure.

My secretary's voice came over the intercom. "Joey is here to see you."

I held the button down. "Send him in."

"Will do."

Joey walked in a second later, but he didn't look like himself. He seemed irritable and down, like he just lost a big hand in poker to an enemy. He placed a folder on my desk then put his hands in his pockets. "Those are the contracts. Let me know if you need anything else." He nodded then made his way toward the door.

"Joey?"

He turned back around. "Hmm?"

"Everything alright?" He was a shadow of his former self.

"I'm fine." He turned back to the door. "See you later."

I knew he was full of it. "Joey, sit down."

He released a very loud sigh before he turned back to me. "I'm just having a bad day. It's nothing worth talking about."

"Sit." I sat in the chair beside him.

His eyes still held his irritation. He sank into the chair next to me.

"What's going on?" We usually told each other everything. I wouldn't say we were best friends, but we were close. We both knew so much about each other that it was hard to keep things hidden.

"Amy dumped me." He stared straight ahead and rested his fingers on his lips, his usual stance.

"Did she say why?" I was bummed to hear this news. I'd hoped that Joey found a nice girl to settle down with. *Apparently, not.*

"No, she didn't." He shrugged. "I've dated so many girls in this city and there's either something I don't like about them or something they don't like about me. There's never any middle ground. I give up. I actually give up."

"Don't say that," I said. "Just because it didn't work out before doesn't mean it won't work out someday."

"Well, I'm tired of putting my heart through this to find out." There was sadness and bitterness in his voice. "Finding the right woman is impossible and I don't want to deal with it anymore. Now I need to find someone to settle down with so my parents will get off my back, someone I can call a friend and have decent sex with. Then I can stop worrying about it."

I cocked an eyebrow at his words and wondered where this was going. But I didn't ask.

He shrugged. "Well, thanks for listening."

"You're discouraged right now but it will get better."

"You want to know the interesting thing?" he asked, slightly smiling. "I have absolutely no problem getting laid by the hottest girls. But I can't find a single girlfriend that I want to stick around." He rested his chin on his knuckles and shook his head slightly. "Love is the dumbest thing I've ever heard and I don't believe in it."

"Well, you're wrong." I said it without thinking. Ethan and I had a volatile and explosive relationship that caused us to be irrational and presumptuous but that didn't mean we didn't love each other. Because we did. "When you find it, you'll understand."

He released a faint chuckle. "I'm done looking. Sorry, Kat."

I kept my hands to myself and didn't comfort him.

He stood up then straightened his shirt. "I need to get going. I'll see you around."

For a moment, I thought he was going to propose the idea of marriage again. I assumed that was where his speech was going. But he didn't bring it up. He seemed to accept my relationship with Cato, and it seemed like he was really over me. I was grateful for that but I wish he had someone to love. I wished reality wasn't spitting him out so aggressively. It was hard for me to believe that a woman would ever dump Joey. Not only was he good-looking and charming, but he was sweet and thoughtful. And for the superficial girls, he came from wealth. There was no better guy in my book. "I'll see you."

"Hey." He turned back to me. "Want to grab dinner tonight?"

Since he was going through a hard time I couldn't say no. "Sure."

***

Cato called me the second I walked through the door. "Milkshake?"

"That name is stuck like glue, isn't it?"

"It's a good name," he said. "I really like it." The smile was in his voice. "So, how about you and me grab some grub?"

"I wish I could but I'm having dinner with Joey."

There was a long pause over the phone. "Why?"

"Amy dumped him. I want to be his personal cheerleader. He seemed really down about it."

"Yeah...I'm sure he was."

Cato had a dark tone and I wasn't sure where it came from. "Do you not like Joey?"

"He wants to marry you. Why would I like him?"

"But he's over me."

He laughed but it was clear he wasn't being humorous. "Yeah right. Don't fall for his bullshit, Katarina."

I didn't like his attitude. "Last time I checked, you weren't my boyfriend. So you should knock off this jealousy."

"I'm not jealous," he argued. "But this guy is desperate to play any card he has. Don't trust him."

"He's been my friend since I can remember. Of course I trust him."

"And I *am* your boyfriend," he snapped. "You don't see anyone but me."

"Are my parents okay?" I said sarcastically.

"I'm not telling you not to see him." He kept his voice low but it was full of irritation. "Do whatever you want. I'm just telling you his intentions toward you are anything but friendly. He'll try to manipulate you in whatever way he can."

"He thinks I'm with you, Cato."

"And he made it pretty clear in your office that he thinks we're just a fling, like all the others you've had. I'm telling you, Joey thinks he has a chance with you, and I promise you he's trying to figure out how to get it."

"Well, you have nothing to worry about."

"I know I don't," he said defensively. "Why would you go for a nutbag when you have a real man to please you?"

"You haven't done any pleasing."

"You have the worst memory in the world, woman."

"Sorry?"

"Nothing," he said quickly. "Where are you guys going?"

"There's this diner he and I frequent. It's like our place."

"That fifties place on sixth?"

"Yeah," I said.

"They have good fries there."

"Why do you think it's our place?" I asked with a smile.

"Can I come over and watch *The Bachelorette* with you when you finish?"

I didn't see the harm in that. "Sure."

"Awesome. I'll be waiting." He hung up.

He never said goodbye before he ended the call and it irritated me. I never knew when the conversation was over until it was already gone.

***

Joey seemed to be in a better mood. He was smiling and making jokes. And he ate all his food, so I assumed he had an appetite. He discussed his most recent golf match against his father. "I creamed him. I mean, it wasn't even a match, really."

"Be nice to your father. He's a sweetheart."

"Oh, I'm nice to him. I just beat him." He ate a few more fries while he laughed. "So, how's it going with you and Cato?" His tone of voice was the same, like he wasn't angry or jealous.

"Good," I said. "We're having a great time together."

"Cato told me something interesting the other day…"

"What's that?" I asked.

"He said he was going to marry you."

I was surprised Cato told him that before I made the plans to actually announce it. But I guess he wanted a jumpstart so the proposal wasn't completely out of the blue. "Yeah?"

"And you didn't know?" he asked.

"We love each other…I guess I assumed that was where it was headed."

"But you didn't tell him about Ethan?" His brow was raised like he was suspicious.

I shrugged. "No man wants to hear about an old lover."

157

He ate a few more fries and kept his gaze downturned. Then he returned his look to me. "Well, considering the fact Ethan is the reason you swore you would never love again, I'm shocked he didn't come up." He studied my face, watching my reaction.

"I told him about it last week. He was very sympathetic."

"I told him in the office that day," he said. "I assumed he already knew. I'm sorry."

"It's okay," I said. "I was going to tell him anyway."

"I'm sorry, but I just find this odd…"

"What so odd about me falling in love and moving on?" I asked.

"Because I know you," he said quickly. "This is such a change of heart I have whiplash. What is it about this guy that's given you new hope?"

I shrugged. "I can't really explain it. There was nothing specific about Ethan that I loved. I just did. It's the same way with Cato."

He nodded and kept eating. "It's just…nevermind."

"What?" I asked. He seemed so incredulous.

"I just assumed that if you did move on, it would be with me."

Were we seriously going to have this conversation again?

"Not for the reason you're thinking," he said immediately, catching my unease. "I assumed Ethan would want you to be with me. He and I were close and he knew I really cared about you. I just figured…forget I said anything."

Ethan and Joey did get along, and Ethan did have a lot of nice things to say about him. Every time he would deploy, he would ask Joey to look after me. "But I can't choose who I love."

"So you love Cato?" he pressed.

"Of course I do." I hated being interrogated like this.

He continued to watch me. "I've known you my whole life and I know when you're lying. But perhaps I'm wrong. I hope I am." He looked down at his food and finally dropped the subject.

Cato was wrong about Joey. Joey wasn't trying to get together with me and didn't seem romantically interested in me anymore. He was just hurt he was being lied to. I didn't know what to say so I let the conversation evaporate.

Joey looked over my shoulder then sighed. "Looks like Cato brought backup."

"Sorry?"

Joey nodded over my shoulder.

When I turned, I saw Cato and his friends sitting at a nearby table. They were all looking this way, casting silent threats at Joey. I faced forward and covered my face. "Oh my god..." This was absolutely humiliating.

"It's safe to say your boyfriend doesn't trust me— one bit."

"I'm sorry," I said. "I told him we were coming here but I didn't think he would show up like a freak."

"And this is the guy you love?" Doubt was in his voice.

I grabbed the saltshaker then threw it at Cato. "You're an asshole, you know that?"

The salt bounced on the table then flew between Cato and Troy, landing on the floor behind them.

"Well, you just gave us good luck," Cato said with a smirk.

I glared at him. "You have a lot of nerve."

"I know I do." That cocky smirk was on his face. "But me and my boys just wanted to get some food. It's a free country, right?"

"Exactly," I said. "And I'm free to do what I want with who I want."

"Don't mind us." He waved me away. "We aren't eavesdropping."

The other four guys gave Joey looks of death, threatening him without the use of words.

"I'm so sorry," I said to Joey. "I'm really embarrassed, if that makes a difference."

"Don't be embarrassed," he said. "Cato is the one who should be embarrassed."

"I won't let them hurt you," I said. "Don't worry about that."

"I'm not scared of them," he said with a cracked voice.

"When it's five on one, I'd be scared of them too."

"It's fine," he said. "You got a jealous man on your hands."

"He's just protective..." I tried to make an excuse for Cato's behavior.

"Ethan was never jealous," he pointed out. "And neither am I."

"I'm not going to compare them," I said immediately. "That's not fair to either one of them."

He sipped his coffee then put the cash down on the table. "Want to get out of here?"

"Please."

We left the booth then walked right past Cato and his friends.

Cato snatched me and yanked me into his lap. "Hey, beautiful." He leaned in and tried to kiss me.

I slapped him instead. It was light and didn't inflict any pain. It was just to make a statement. "Perhaps you didn't pick up on this but I don't put up with bullshit. If you act like this again, we're through."

"Ouch," Troy whispered beside him.

"I'm just looking out for you," Cato said. "I don't trust that weasel over there."

"That weasel is my friend," I said. "And don't ever insult my friend again."

He kept his hand on my waist but his eyes burned in irritation. "Call me when you're done with him."

"No, I won't be calling you tonight." I moved out of his lap. "You can call me when you grow up."

***

Cato called me a few times around nine o' clock but I didn't answer. I let it go to voicemail and didn't plan on listening to any messages he left. My irritation was at its peak. If he didn't want to get slapped again, he should leave me alone.

Then there was a knock on the door. "Girl Scout cookies." It was clearly a male trying to do a female's voice. And it did not go over well. I didn't even need to look through the peephole to know it was Cato.

"Go away. I'm not interested in buying anything you have to sell."

Cato spoke normally. "Baby, please open the door."

"Stop calling me baby," I argued. "I'm *not* your baby."

"Milkshake, open the door."

"Don't call me that either," I snapped.

"Why?" he asked. "It's such a cute nickname." There was a smile in his voice and I could hear it through the door. "Come on, open the door. Let me apologize to your face."

"I'm not ready to hear you apologize."

"Cut me some slack," he said. "I'm really into you. You can't get mad about that."

"Watch me."

"I wish I could," he said. "But there's a big slab of wood in the way—and I'm not referring to my dick."

I rolled my eyes. "You think being a pervert is going to get me to forgive you?"

"No. But it'll make you smile."

"Unbelievable..." I muttered under my breath.

"Are you referring to me?"

I growled. "Just go away, Cato."

"Okay, I politely asked you to open the door and I'm getting sick of arguing like this." The knob started to turn as he picked it. Then the lock came undone and he stepped inside.

"Did you just break into my apartment?" I hissed.

He held up a paperclip and a knife. "It's a handy trick. I'll teach you so you can break into my apartment whenever you like."

"Because I really want to do that..."

He put the thief tools in his pocket then came close to me. "Here's my formal apology. I'm sorry."

"Why did you go down there to begin with?" I demanded.

"I'm telling you, I don't trust Joey," he said. "I just wanted him to know that he's got five pairs of eyes on him, not just one."

"Are you a child?" I demanded. "Because you're acting like a high school bully."

"Hey, I didn't threaten him or touch him. I just looked at him."

"And direct eye-contact is a sigh of hostility and danger."

He looked deep into my eyes. "Or physical attraction..."

"Stop joking around, Cato. I'm not your girlfriend and I don't put up with jealous guys. It's annoying."

"I'm not jealous," he repeated. "I said this at least ten times now. I don't trust him. Period. That was my subtle way of telling him I'm onto his plan."

"And what plan is that?" I crossed my arms over my chest.

"He says he broke up with Amy and now he's so heartbroken that he'll never love again. He doesn't want a serious relationship again, just something convenient. Tell me if I'm hot or cold."

He was burning hot. And that was a little freaky. "How did you know that?"

"Because I'm not stupid," he snapped. "He's trying to make you think he's over you so you'll agree to marry him."

"Even if that were true I already agreed to try to have something with you. So, why do you care?"

"Just because I don't like the guy doesn't mean I don't think he's intelligent and determined. When someone has an edge like he does, being a good friend to you, he could discreetly manipulate you."

"Well, he didn't bring up marriage to me again."

"Because he's playing it cool. Trust me."

"No." I stepped back and sat on the couch. "I don't believe that. Maybe Joey does still want me but he would never trick me into something."

"You obviously don't understand how crazy in love he is."

I sighed then stared at the blank TV screen.

Cato sat beside me then moved his hand to my thigh. "I'm sorry and I won't let it happen again, okay?"

"Yeah?"

"Yeah." He squeezed my thigh playfully. "And you are my girlfriend so I am entitled to be a little jealous." He held up his forefinger and thumb, keeping them less than an inch apart. "Just a smudge."

His cuteness was weighing me down and I couldn't fight it.

He leaned toward me. "I see that smile in your eyes."

"There's no smile," I lied. I felt my lips twitch.

He smiled in victory. "Sure..."

I looked away so our faces weren't so close together.

Cato grabbed my chin then forced my mouth to his. He kissed me hard, claiming me without the use of words. His lips brush past mine with a warm fluidity, and then he slipped his tongue into my mouth, exciting me almost instantly. "Forgive me?" he said as he continued to kiss me. He laid me down on the couch and moved over me.

My hands dug into his hair and moved down his back, feeling every line of muscle.

"Baby?" he asked as he kept kissing me.

I kept going and wrapped my legs around his waist.

He broke our kiss then fisted my hair. He dominated me, forcing me to look at him. "I asked you a question." There was command in his eyes, and even if I were a Roman soldier, I would obey.

"Yes."

He kissed me again. "Good."

E. L. Todd

Cato

River slid into the booth across from me with his beer in hand. "I got two chicks who are willing to get down and dirty. They are both brunettes and they got gorgeous racks. Am I the king or what?" He took a deep drink then wiped the foam off his mouth.

I had no idea what he was talking about. "What two chicks?"

"For our group fuck," he explained. "Remember? We wanted to do something different since threesomes are getting old."

Now it came back to me. "Dude, you know I'm seeing Katarina."

"You're actually serious with this girl?" he asked. "I thought you were just hanging out with her because you're a weirdo that can't let go of the fact she doesn't remember you."

I gave him a deep glare. "No."

"You're sleeping with her?"

"No."

"Then what is going on?" he asked.

"We're dating."

River sighed then took another drink. "Are you trying to put us all on unemployment?"

"She's not like that. She would never throw us under the bus. That happened one time. Get over it."

"When my job is on the line, I won't get over it."

"I'll have her terminate the agreement then I'll escort her privately."

"Thank you," he said. "Do it soon. Like, today."

"I'll ask her next time I see her."

"You better, asshole."

I rested my arm over the back of the chair and looked out the window.

"So, how is it going with her?"

"Good."

"She still has no idea you already fucked?"

"Nope." It still didn't make sense to me. How could she not remember someone she slept with?

"Maybe she has some sort of medical condition."

"I don't think so," I said. "She's never forgetful about anything else."

"Hmm..." He rubbed his chin while he remained in thought.

"She used to be married." I hadn't told any of the guys this, but if my relationship was going to go somewhere I had to tell them. I didn't want them to make a bad joke about the Army or widows and make her upset.

"Say what?" he asked, leaning back. "When?"

"Five years ago."

He started to count on his fingers. "How old was she? Twelve?"

"Nineteen. They weren't together for long."

"People who get married young usually divorce."

"Actually, she's a widow." It made me sad to think about. Losing someone you loved must be unbearable. Fortunately, I'd never experienced anything like that. "He was in the military and he was killed in the line of duty."

"Holy shit." He leaned over the table and remained quiet for a few moments. "I'm not trying to be insensitive but are you sure you want to get involved in that? She probably has a lot of baggage."

I shook my head. "I really like her, River. I just do. I don't know why because she doesn't even remember me but I do. When I'm not with her, she's all I think about. It's not ideal to be with someone who's already been married but...it is what it is."

"If you're sure..."

"He's been gone for five years so she's moved on. She's not crying every other minute, and when she talks about him she actually smiles. It's not like she's still grieving."

"I guess I just assumed when I settled down with the one, I would be the one to her too," he said with a shrug.

It was difficult for me to describe my relationship with Katarina because most of my thoughts couldn't be explained in words. Most of the time there were just feelings. "I think I could be the one to her."

"Wouldn't her husband have been the one?" he asked.

"He might have been but...she was really young. I'm sure they loved each other but she and I...we have something special. Our conversations flow like water, and we have this natural reaction to one another...I can't explain it."

"Yeah...you can't."

"I just feel like we're a perfect match."

"How so?" he asked.

"Because we met two years ago, in a crowd of millions of people in a tiny area. I was there at the right place and the right time. So was she. And then...she becomes my client. Seriously, what are the odds of that?"

He gave me a serious look. "You know I love you, man, but you're talking crazy right now. I sincerely hope you aren't putting in all this effort for this one girl solely because you already slept with her and she doesn't remember. Is this about your pride?"

"No," I snapped. "It's not. When we hooked up I felt something then too. I wanted to see her again, to take her on a real date. That's never happened to me before, and now I have another chance. I know it doesn't make any sense but that's the truth."

"What? Are you saying she's your soul mate or something?" Skepticism was heavy in his voice.

"No...but I think we're meant to be together."

River sighed and I could tell he made his best effort not to roll his eyes. "Come on, Cato. When did you start pulling all this shit out of your ass? This girl is turning your world upside down."

"I'm being serious. What are the odds of us meeting twice? She didn't even live here the first time we met."

"But she doesn't remember you." He said each word slowly, trying to make each word sink into my brain. "How can she be meant for you if you're so forgetful?"

"There's got to be a reason why she doesn't remember me," I said. "And it has nothing to do with me not being memorable. I had a great time that night. There's no way she didn't."

"If she did, why didn't she leave a phone number?" he questioned.

I shrugged. "She said she would never date again and she was abiding by that rule. I think if she had an open mind about me, she would fall hard. And I'm pretty sure she's starting to."

River was still incredulous but he didn't repeat his argument. "So, no group fuck?"

"No. Sorry."

"Lame."

I chuckled. "Ask Jett. He'd do it in a heartbeat."

"Yeah, maybe. But I figured if I was going to see one of you guys naked, it would be you."

I cocked an eyebrow. "Should I be worried...?"

He chuckled. "You just seem like you're more open-minded."

Even if Katarina wasn't in my life I wasn't sure if I could do that. Threesomes and foursomes were fine but with another dude...not exactly appealing.

River rubbed the back of his neck. "Weasel still sniffing around?"

I really disliked that guy. "I know what he's doing but Kat won't believe it. She says they're too good of friends. I'm not buying it."

"Well, she's never wanted to date him before so I doubt she'll change her mind," he reasoned. "Unless he holds her down and—"

"Don't say that." It made me sick to think about.

"Don't stress about him," he said. "That's all I'm trying to say."

"I'll try." I took a long drink of my beer then looked out the window. "Kat doesn't appreciate my protectiveness and jealousy. But she needs to understand—" Across the street, I thought I saw Joey lurking behind a car. He held a pair of binoculars to his eyes and he was scoping me out through the bar window.

Did I really just see that?

River waited for me to finish the sentence, and when I didn't, he followed my gaze out the window. "What's up? What do you see?"

"That fucking weasel." When I realized my mind wasn't playing tricks on me, I snapped. I wanted to turn the table over, break it into pieces, and then chase him down with a long stick of wood.

River narrowed his eyes. "He's watching you?"

"He's behind the blue Volvo. He's wearing black."

"Fuck, it is that weasel."

I slid out of the booth. "Now I'm breaking his face."

River followed me, ready for a fight. "I'll hold and you punch."

"That won't be necessary," I said with a clenched jaw. "I want to do both." I jogged across the street and heard the sounds of horns from the taxis and cars. River was right behind me. When I reached the sidewalk, Joey realized what was happening. At a sprint, he took off down the sidewalk.

"You're dead!" I chased after him and fantasized about what I would do when I snatched him. The sidewalk with packed with a crowd, and maneuvering through them was difficult. Joey was twenty feet ahead, and he reached the corner of the street then waved down a cab.

"I don't think so, motherfucker." I kept running, needing to get to him before the cab took off.

I didn't make it. Joey shut the door and then the cab pulled onto the street.

"Fuck!" I punched a nearby pole and cursed again.

River caught up to me, out of breath. "Why is he tailing you?"

"I have no fucking idea." I ran my fingers through my hair, distressed. "But it can't be good. He's trying to get dirt on me. I can't think of any other reason."

"We should have ripped his arms and legs off in that diner."

"It's never too late," I said darkly.

"Are you going to tell Kat about this?"

I should. She should know that the man she considered to be her best friend was a fucking psychopath. He was so obsessed with her that he was borderline crazy. But I knew that would be pointless. "She wouldn't believe me anyway."

***

When I arrived at her door, she gave me a bright smile that reached her eyes. It was clear she wasn't still upset with me over my fiasco with Joey, and all was forgiven. If I brought up my last encounter with him, it would certainly spoil the evening.

My hands moved to her waist and I gave her a hard kiss on the mouth. She reciprocated with the same enthusiasm, and her hands went to my chest. She touched it often so I assumed it was her favorite feature. That was fine by me. My favorite feature was the same area, just on her.

I slowly pulled away and looked down into her face. "Did you take a professional kissing class? Because you're good at it."

"I guess I've just had lots of practice," she said with a smile.

I grabbed a handful of her hair then yanked her head back, exposing her throat. I placed a few kisses on her neck and listened to her moan. "And why does your skin always taste so sweet? You practice that too?"

"I guess I eat a lot of fruit."

I released her hair and towered over her. "Ready?"

"Uh...sure."

I smirked. "What's your hesitance?"

"Well, when you kiss me like that I don't want to go anywhere."

I chuckled. "Let's save the fooling around for later. Otherwise, we'll never get out of here."

"Good point."

We left her apartment and headed to Beautiful Entourage.

"Where are we going?" she asked.

"I need you to sign some termination papers." I held her hand as we walked up the sidewalk, like a regular couple.

"Termination papers?"

"I can't escort you anymore, not when we're romantically involved like this."

"So...what will I do?" There was fear in her voice.

"I'll do it for free. Don't worry about it."

"But, you can't pose as my husband if you're dating me. That could get weird."

I shrugged. "I have to do this, baby. The guys are really concerned about it."

She nodded. "I guess I understand."

"We'll figure it out though," I said. "And maybe I shouldn't pose as your husband at all. Let's just see where this relationship goes first."

"Okay..." There was a deep sadness to her voice.

"What's wrong?" I watched her face.

"I just...nevermind."

"Tell me," I pressed. I pulled her further into my side.

"I'm not sure if I ever want to get married again—for real," she said. "It's just...I don't know."

"How about we just take it slow and see where this goes?" I asked. I noticed that when we talked about her hesitance, it made her more hesitant. But when we just lived in the moment, she was more accepting to change.

"Okay."

We went inside the office and she signed all the paperwork. Once that was done, I was a free man. I was no longer legally prohibited from sleeping with her. I wasn't planning on it anytime soon anyway, but it was still a relief. Now I was just her boyfriend.

"Well, this is a good start to a date," she teased.

I put my arm around her waist as we headed to Times Square. "I'll make up for it as the night goes on."

"Oh, I'm sure you will."

We reached Times Square and walked down the sidewalk. I watched her face, wondering if she was reliving any memories. I wanted her to realize we'd already met in our past but her mind was completely closed off. Was she on drugs that night? "Do you go to Times Square on New Year's Eve?" I asked casually. Maybe I could jog her memory a little bit.

"I've been once," she said.

So, she remembered the night, just not me. "Have fun?"

"Yeah. But it was freezing cold and there were a million people there. If a fight broke out, it would be a terrible stampede."

I nodded and kept walking. "Did you go with friends?"

"Yeah, two of them." She looked at a newspaper stand as she passed and her mind seemed to be elsewhere.

"Would you go again?"

She shrugged. "Maybe."

"Meet any cool people?" *Come on, woman. How can you not remember me?*

She didn't look at me as she kept walking. "No."

Burn. I wanted to growl but I kept it back.

"Where do you want to eat?"

I stopped in front of a Thai place. "How does this place sound?"

"Great," she said. "I'm starving so I'll say yes to pretty much anything."

"Really?" I gave her a dark smolder. "*Anything*?"

She rolled her eyes but smiled at the same time. "I meant in terms of food."

"I can give you something to eat." My lips moved to her jaw and I nibbled her gently.

She froze and her eyes became lidded with pleasure.

When I pulled away, I liked the dazed look on her face. The sexual attraction between us was equal. I wanted her as much as she wanted me, if not more so. Our relationship was exactly the same as it was two years ago. How different would our lives be if I'd just gotten her number? Would I still be her boyfriend? Or would I be something more? I'd never been marriage material, hardly boyfriend material, but the idea of making that kind of commitment didn't scare me. It just convinced me even more that she was the one.

We entered the restaurant then took our seats. She pulled her hair over one shoulder before she picked up the menu. One side of her neck was exposed, and all I could think about was sucking the skin until it was raw. Flashbacks of our heated night came back to me. I was desperate to take her on my sheets but I was also nervous. Would it be a replay of last time? Or would she stick around?

She put her menu down when she made her selection. "I'm getting Thai iced tea."

"Good choice. It's a little too sweet for me, however."

"You're missing out," she said. "I have a sweet tooth."

"Do you like Oreos?" I blurted.

"It's my favorite cookie," she said immediately.

She really didn't remember her New Year's resolution she shared with me? I had to protect my pride so she wouldn't completely demolish it. But it was becoming difficult.

We placed our order then stared at each other across the table. I never grew bored of looking at her exquisite face. She was gorgeous and flawless. I'd been with a long line of women, most of them models, but they couldn't compare to Katarina. The slight curve of her lips always enticed me to devour her, and the subtle brightness of her eyes, always constant, had my attention endlessly. She was a small woman, exceptionally short and tiny, but she took up the whole room with her personality, wit, and attitude. Was this how Rhett felt when he met Aspen? He talked about her before they got together, and he said he just knew. Was this how Troy felt too? Was I breaking every rule just like them because I'd found the right girl? I hoped so. I already had one chance with her and I blew it. I didn't want to blow it again.

"Cato?"

"Hmm?" *Did she say something?*

A slow smile stretched her lips. "I've been trying to get your attention for the past minute and you've just been staring at me blankly..."

"Oh...sorry." I didn't even notice.

"What was distracting you so much?" Judging the joy on her face, she already knew.

I leaned over the table and rested my elbows on the surface. "It's a secret. Come closer."

She leaned forward, her face close to mine.

"This is what I was thinking about." I pressed my lips to hers gently and immediately felt that cosmic electricity. Her lips were full and soft, and they tasted delicious. I wanted to take all of her and treasure her all night long.

The waiter's voice came into our ears. "Um...here is your dinner."

Katarina tried to pull away but I held her in place. Then I held one finger to the waiter, telling him I wasn't finished. I finished my kiss before I leaned back into my chair. "Now we're done."

E. L. Todd

The waiter gave a half-asked smile but it was clear he was extremely annoyed. He placed the dishes in front of us before he walked away and took care of his other tables.

Katarina had a tint to her cheeks. Her eyes were downcast as she inserted her fork into her noodles but there was still a visible smile on her lips. "You're going to get us kicked out."

"Nah. I'm not leaving until I eat."

She got the noodles in her mouth but there was one that was particularly long. She sucked it into her mouth until it disappeared.

The action fascinated me and I kept thinking about it even after she was finished. I remembered the way she gave me head. It was amazing. She used both hands and jerked me off like a pro. My cock hardened in my jeans and I wish it would remain soft. There would only be one thing on my mind if I were walking around with a hard dick.

"Isn't it funny how we are together considering the fact we use to dislike each other?"

"You never disliked me," I argued.

"No, I did," she said with a laugh. "Your insults were annoying."

"You still thought I was hot."

"Irrelevant."

"I don't think so," I argued.

"Anyway, I'd really like to know why you disliked me." She watched my face as she said it. "And you better not say it was because I was too pretty or some shit like that."

I tried not to laugh. "I don't want to say."

"Why not?" she asked. "I have a thick skin."

"It's not insulting."

"Then tell me."

I looked down at my food as I ate. "I'll tell you. But not now."

"Then when?"

"I don't know...but I will."

Both of her eyebrows were raised. "Why are you being so mysterious?"

"You'll understand when I tell you."

"But—"

"Baby, just trust me on this." I gave her a firm look. "Be patient."

She sighed then looked down at her food. "Fine."

"Good girl."

She kicked me under the table. "Don't talk to me like I'm a dog."

"Why?" I asked. "Dogs are cute. I love dogs."

That cute smile stretched her lips again. "I love dogs too."

"See, we're meant for each other."

"Because we both love dogs?" she asked with a laugh.

"It's pretty important." I kept eating and tried not to chuckle at the incredulous look on her face. Somehow, she looked really cute when she was confused.

She dropped the subject and kept eating, probably not seeing the logic in continuing the conversation.

When we finished dinner, I grabbed the tab.

She snatched it out of my grasp. "I'm buying this time."

I gave her a, "Don't fuck with me look," and snatched it back. "No. I pay for your meals. Don't go all feminist on me."

"I *am* a feminist," she said in offense.

"Well, I'm not. I pay for your things."

"Excuse me?" she said. "You aren't a feminist?"

"I believe women can do anything men can do. But I also think I need to take care of you. And that's what's going to happen. I guess I believe in chivalry more than feminism."

"And I believe in an equal partnership."

I threw the cash inside and let the tab on the table. "Well, I don't. Get used to it."

She narrowed her eyes at me.

"That's the kind of man I am, sweetheart. We can argue about it all you want. I don't mind because you're really cute when you get fired up and angry but it won't change anything."

Katarina still looked pissed but she didn't tell me off. "If you weren't so hot and sweet..."

I smiled. "Good thing I am." I left my chair then helped her out of hers. Then I hugged her waist as we walked out.

She was stiff beside me but I knew her anger would slowly disappear. We walked up the sidewalk and I maneuvered us to a place we'd already been. The convenient store looked exactly as it used to two years ago.

I stopped and turned toward the door. "I'm going to pick up a few things before we head back."

"Like what?" she asked.

"A snack." I walked inside with her then headed to the cookie aisle. I discreetly watched her face, hoping to see some sign of recognition. I stopped in front of the Oreos then grabbed a few.

"You really love Oreos, huh?" she asked with a light laugh.

My plan wasn't working. She didn't remember anything. "Yeah. And I want to eat them off your body when we get home."

"Ooh...that sounds fun."

I paid for the Oreos then we walked outside. A bum wasn't leaning against the wall like last time but the night seemed pretty similar to two years ago. The neon sign on the roof made a constant buzzing noise, and a swarm of moths danced in the light.

I grabbed Katarina and pushed her against the wall of the convenient store then kissed her hard. My hands moved slightly under her shirt and I felt the soft skin of her stomach. I devoured her, desperately trying to get her to remember that night. It meant something to me. I had to know it meant something to her. Connections were rare, if not impossible, for me to experience. I couldn't let her take that away from me.

Her fingers dug into my hair and she twisted the strands while she kissed me. She breathed hard into my mouth, and my kisses stifled her moans. I was hard, and I let her know that by pressing it against her.

"You're so beautiful," I said between kisses. I didn't say this last time but I was thinking it. This girl was driving me up the wall and I was still fighting for her. It would make sense for me to give up and walk away. She was already married once before, she had a psycho friend that wanted her to himself, and she had the worst memory on the face of the planet. But here I was, still obsessed and working my ass off to keep this girl around.

What the hell was wrong with me?

When our embrace got too heated, I ended the kiss and pressed my forehead against hers. "You want to head back to your place?"

"Yeah...we need to eat those cookies."

"I was thinking the same thing."

***

We sat at the kitchen table and opened the plastic boxes of cookies. I grabbed the same flavors we tried out last time. The root beer ones sat there uneaten. I already knew I didn't like the taste and neither did she. But I'd eat them if it made her realize who I was.

"Try these." I pushed the root beer ones toward her.

She cringed. "No, thanks." She grabbed an original one and took a bite.

"Why not?"

"They're gross."

"I think they're gross too."

She narrowed her eyes in confusion while she chewed her cookie. "Then why did you buy them?"

I shrugged. "I thought you might like them."

She shook her head quickly. "Can't stand the taste."

"When did you try them?" *Will she remember that?*

"A few years ago. I didn't care for them."

I wanted to scream. How could she not recognize my face? We were only together for a few hours but she really forgot about me? Why did I remember her but she didn't remember me? I tried not to get mad and take it out on her. I ate a vanilla flavored one and tried to figure out how I would get her to remember me. It seemed impossible at this point.

"What's your problem?" she asked.

"Problem? I don't have a problem." I looked down at my hands as I said it. I was doing a piss of a job hiding my annoyance.

"You just got moody all of a sudden."

"You're seeing things that aren't there," I lied.

"I think you're full of it. But if you don't want to tell me, that's your right."

I ate another cookie and thought about my next plan.

"Excuse me for a moment." She left the table and walked into her bedroom.

Once she was gone, I leaned back into the chair and released a sigh. Why was this bothering me so much? Why couldn't I just let it go? If she did remember me from that night, it might actually hurt the relationship rather than help it. So why couldn't I let it go? I had no fucking idea. Maybe River was right. It was just because of my wounded pride.

Katarina opened the door, and she wasn't wearing the dress she had on earlier. She wore a black baby doll top that barely reached her thighs. And stockings were on her legs slightly above her knee.

I froze, holding an Oreo in my hand without any intention of eating it.

She gave me a seductive grin. "Want to see my bedroom?" She twisted a strand of dark hair in her fingertips, being flirty.

"Uh…" I couldn't remember how to talk. The ability left me. My tongue felt swollen and useless in my mouth.

She lifted her hand then beckoned me toward her with her forefinger. "Come on. I'm a little cold and need someone to keep me warm."

"Uh…" I sounded like an idiot but couldn't do much else. I'd already seen her naked and I knew she was a heathen in bed, but seeing her wear slutty black lingerie impaired me. She looked damn fine and I wanted to rip everything off with my teeth.

"I'll be waiting." She walked back inside her bedroom.

Once she was gone and I couldn't see her gorgeous legs, my brain started working again. I didn't want to have sex just yet, not when she might hurt me again, but I couldn't resist her when she dressed like that. My cock was hard in my jeans and telling me to march into that bedroom right this second. But my mind was telling me it wasn't a good idea.

The head of my cock made the decision for me.

I entered her bedroom and saw her lying on the bed. Her legs were leaning against her headboard, parallel to the wall, and her back was on the bed. She tilted her head back so she could look at me.

"What took you so long?" she said.

I smirked then crawled over her. Our heads were opposite of each other, my chin near her head. "It took me a moment to recover from the shock. You look fucking hot."

"I'm sure an experienced man like you has seen better."

My eyes turned serious as I looked at her beautiful face. "Actually, I haven't."

"Oh really?" she challenged. But there was a playful glow in her blue eyes.

"Really." My voice came out quiet but it contained my sincerity. I lowered myself to my elbows and kept my head over hers. I'd never been in this position with a girl but I liked it. I leaned over her and pressed my lips to hers. Her bottom lip was on top, and I sucked it like I couldn't get enough. My hands moved in her hair, cradling her head. And I continued to kiss her.

Her arms moved over her shoulders and she gripped the back of my neck, deepening the kiss.

Our quiet breathing became louder the longer we kissed, and I enjoyed the feel of her small tongue as it moved past mine. When I opened my eyes, I could see the cleavage line of her breasts. I resisted the urge to grab a tit and squeeze it. Kissing her was enough to satisfy me and I enjoyed that instead. Kissing was usually the activity I enjoyed the least. I preferred to skip all the bases and head straight to home plate. But with Katarina, the smallest things were enough.

An hour passed and we made out quietly on her bed. Her breathing fell on my chin, and my fingers dug deep into her silky hair. I wanted to do this all night and never stop. I wanted this to last a lifetime.

Katarina grabbed the fabric of my shirt and pulled it over my head. It messed up my hair as it was yanked away. I didn't mind if she wanted to see me shirtless but I didn't want this to go anywhere. I liked what we had.

She reached behind her neck and untied her halter-top. Then she pulled it down, revealing her perky and round tits. Her nipples were hard and I wanted to suck them. I stared at them because I couldn't help myself. My hand grabbed one and massaged it aggressively. Then I rubbed my thumb across her nipple. I'd already seen them but I'd forgotten just how hot they were.

She moved her hands tip her hips and grabbed her thong. Then she started to pull it down.

If I let this go too far, I wouldn't be able to restrain myself from sliding into home plate. I grabbed her hand and steadied it. Every guy in the world would think I was a pussy for stopping her but I didn't care.

Her lips became immobile then she stopped kissing me altogether.

"Let's take this slow," I whispered.

"We've known each other for two months."

Longer, actually. "I'm not ready."

She sat up and faced me, her rack still in my line of sight. "How is that possible? You strike me as the kind of guy who doesn't like to wait."

"Because I'm not," I said bluntly. "But we both know I'm different with you."

Her eyes softened.

"But that doesn't mean we can't do other things." I crawled over her then lowered her head onto a pillow. "I can make you come in many other ways."

Her eyes lit up in desire. "Yeah?"

"You want me to prove it?"

"Please." Her arms snaked around my neck and she wrapped her legs around my waist.

I had a dark tattoo down my ribs and I didn't have that before. Perhaps if I had when we slept together, she would remember me. But now she was less likely to recognize me.

She pulled my lips to her and kissed me hard. Her legs squeezed my narrow hips, and then her hands moved down my back, dragging her nails against my skin. Even though I still had my jeans on, I knew she could feel my hard-on pressed against her. I kept thinking about her in intense sexual ways and I tried to stop myself. It would only weaken my resolve.

Satisfying her would stifle her desire so she wouldn't try to seduce me anymore. My hand moved her thong over and my fingers found the soft and wet area between her legs. I slowly played with her, building her up until I gave her my best moves. I kissed her as I touched her, and I felt my cock twitch in my jeans.

She was so fucking hot.

Katarina became more aggressive, and her nails dug into me with such pressure I thought they would break the skin. Quiet moans escaped her lips and she breathed hard into my mouth like she couldn't get enough air.

My fingers rubbed her clitoris, moving it in a circular motion. I knew she liked it when she gripped me savagely. Her cries increased, and she was moving against me like she wanted to fuck my brains out.

My fingers slowed down and I touched her lightly, teasing her. The longer I waited, the more intense her climax would be. I'd been around the block a few times and I knew my way around a woman's body. I knew what made them tick.

"Goddammit, Cato." She growled at me but the sound was full of longing.

I tried not to smile. "You want me to make you come?"

"What do you think, asshole?" She kissed me harder and sucked my bottom lip.

I pulled away and gave her a smile. "Alright, I hear ya." I pressed my face to hers and examined her face. "I want to watch you."

She gripped my shoulders and pulled me into her.

My fingers moved her clitoris hard and fast. I wish my tongue was doing it but I didn't want to rush this. I wasn't as excited to get to the finish line because I'd already been there once before. Katarina hadn't, so to speak.

Katarina found her threshold and released a loud yell. "Oh god…" She showed the same enthusiasm last time I made her come. "Cato." But this time she said my name, and I liked that. Her nails dug into me, almost cutting me. And then the orgasm passed and she relaxed her hold. Her breathing was labored, and slowly it returned to normal.

"You're vicious in bed." I looked down into her face, seeing the redness flush her cheeks.

"I just know what I want." She gave me a gentle kiss.

"I can tell."

Her hands moved up my stomach, over my tattoo, and to my chest. "I like your ink."

"Yeah? You should get some too. It would look hot."

"Maybe when I find something I want." She placed a kiss in the center of my chest then rolled me to my back.

I knew what was going to happen. I was hard and wanted to come but I didn't want to do too much, too fast. I grabbed her hands and stopped her from unbuttoning my jeans. "Cuddle with me."

She gave me an incredulous look. "Your dick is about to break your zipper. And you want to cuddle?"

A slow smile stretched my lips. "Don't mind him."

She unbuttoned my jeans anyway.

I grabbed her hands. "You don't owe me anything. Now lay with me."

Her eyebrow shot up. "What's your deal? I'm trying to give you head."

"I just don't want to rush anything."

She still wasn't convinced. "Are you a pussy?"

An involuntary laugh escaped my lips. "No, I'm not. I genuinely like you, so you don't have to suck my dick to keep me around."

"That's not why I'm offering." She unzipped my jeans. "It's because I want to do it." She got my jeans off then pulled down my boxers, revealing my long cock that was happy to see her. "And I've been told I give great head." A flirtatious look was in her eyes.

By me.

She leaned over and took me into her mouth.

That was it. I was gone. I had no interest in being a gentleman and I wanted to come in the back of her throat. I wanted her to take all of me and suck me off.

She used one hand to jerk my length with even strokes and she took me into her mouth at the same time. She slid up and down my cock, just like a pro.

I leaned back and just enjoyed it.

She pulled her hair over one shoulder and deep-throated me, making sucking noises as she did it.

I grabbed her hair and fisted it, keeping it out of her face. Then I guided her up and down, moaning as I did it. Maybe the reason I was obsessed with her was because she gave such amazing head. It wouldn't be that surprising.

After making out with her for an hour, seeing her in lingerie, and watching her come, I didn't have the strength to last long. I wanted to come and feel that warm sensation throughout my entire body.

I tapped the side of her head twice, letting her know I was about to come. If she didn't want to feel my cum in the back of her throat, she needed to pull away now.

Instead, she looked up at me when she continued to go down on me.

Yes. I fisted her hair again and rocked into her mouth from below. My body started to tense in preparation and the most pleasant sensation stretched to every nerve and cell. I pushed my dick further into her as the climax began. "Fuck." I gripped her neck as I released, filling her mouth with my seed. "Mmm…"

Katarina continued to move on my dick, making my orgasm last as long as possible.

When I finally finished, I was in a daze. I was exhausted and satisfied. I lay back on the bed and stared at the ceiling with lidded eyes. I could die right now and I wouldn't care.

"Told you." She got off me then fixed her hair.

"Told me what?" I asked quietly.

"I give good head."

"Oh, yes you do." I grabbed her wrist and pulled her toward me. I positioned her into my side and wrapped my arm tightly around her, holding her like a teddy bear. My lips moved to her hairline and I inhaled her scent.

I felt something while I held her in my arms. It originated somewhere deep inside me, and it burned my skin. It was painful, but it felt good at the same time. I was happy but I was also scared. My heart had weakened in her presence, and it was becoming harder and harder for me to keep her at a distance. I was falling for a girl who may never fall for me. She would probably hurt me like she did last time.

But that didn't stop me.

Katarina

Relaxed and satisfied, I lay in his arms on my bed. My body had experienced a major mound of pleasure, and now all I wanted to do was fall asleep. Cato was excellent in bed, and he wasn't selfish. Sometimes it was hard to find a guy that cared just as much about getting you off as he did about getting himself off.

His lips brushed my hair then he placed a gentle kiss along my hairline.

My eyes were growing lidded, and sleep wanted to take me. My soft sheets enveloped me, making me feel like I was sleeping on a cloud. My eyes were heavy and I fought to keep them open. When I realized I couldn't, I sat up.

I stretched my arms over my head and yawned. "Man, I'm tired." I moved my fingers through the tangles of my hair. Cato's large hand put it in disarray when he gripped it savagely.

"Me too," he said quietly.

I got out of bed and put on a t-shirt and shorts. Then I waited for him to get dressed.

He lay naked on the bed, just staring at me.

What was he doing? Why wasn't he getting dressed?

Cato watched me with equal interest. "Are you coming to bed?"

"If I lay down again, I'll fall asleep."

"Then lay down..." He cocked an eyebrow.

"But I need to walk you out."

His face quickly changed. His dark eyes narrowed as they honed in on my face, and his eyebrows tensed and moved a few inches up. His lips pressed tightly together, making a thin line, and then he sat up and didn't look at me. "Gotcha." He quickly pulled his jeans on and faced the opposite way, giving me his back. Then he pulled on his t-shirt and grabbed his keys and wallet.

His attitude completely changed and I wasn't sure what caused it. He was relaxed just a moment ago. Now he was moving like he couldn't get out of there quick enough. I followed him to the living room and realized he was already at the front door. "Night." He walked out.

"Whoa, wait."

He sighed as he turned to me, clearly annoyed.

"What's wrong?"

He stared at me for several heartbeats, not blinking. "Not a damn thing, sweetheart." His tone was colder than liquid nitrogen.

What was I missing here?

Cato turned away to walk out.

"You aren't going to kiss me goodbye?" I knew there was something wrong but he wouldn't tell me what it was.

"Why?" he asked. "I came over here like a one-night stand and made you come. Now I'll be out of your hair." He bowed deeply, glaring at me as he did it, and then marched off.

"Cato!"

He didn't turn around this time.

I stood in front of the open door and tried to figure out what went wrong. We were lying in bed together, both recovering from the pleasure we gave to one another. Then when I prepared to walk him out, his attitude completely changed. He turned vicious, just like he used to be when we first met.

What did I say?

What did I do?

His last comment echoed in my mind. Did he think I used him? Was he upset I didn't ask him to sleep over? That didn't seem like something a guy would get mad over. But maybe that was it.

I'd never had a guy sleep at my place before, not since Ethan. We fooled around and had our fun, but then I sent them packing directly afterwards. I didn't do sleepovers. It was a habit I hadn't broken.

But would that really make Cato upset?

***

With a distracted mind, it was difficult to get work done. Cato was in my thoughts, and the last words he said to me were permanently ingrained in my ears. While I was signing documents on my computer, I kept thinking about him and marked the wrong date. Then I made another mistake. Stress weighed on me and I wondered if I would be able to finish the workday without messing up again.

A knock sounded on my door. "Can I come in?" It was Joey.

Now wasn't the best time but I'm sure he had something important to say—business wise. "Come in."

He entered then sat in the chair facing my desk. A folder was in his hand. Silently, he stared at me. It was a little creepy, honestly. He didn't speak, and that was just weirder.

"How can I help you?" I finally said.

He tossed the folder on my desk. "A professional escort, huh?"

His words sunk into me and put me on edge. Was he talking about Cato? He knew? How did he figure it out? I decided to play dumb. "Sorry?"

Joey rested his ankle on the opposite knee. A snide smirk stretched one side of his lips. He seemed to be enjoying himself immensely. "You paid Cato to pretend to be your boyfriend. I know everything, Kat."

I kept my poker face and hid my real emotions. The fact he knew my secret could be detrimental. He could tell my entire family and I would be a laughing joke until the day I died. "And how do you know such a thing?"

His grin stretched wider. "It wasn't that difficult. I just did a little digging."

I wanted to smack that smirk right off his face. Actually, I wanted to strangle him. "So you stalked Cato?"

"I didn't stalk him," he corrected. "I just got some information."

Maybe Cato was right about Joey. He was a psychotic and obsessive creep.

He shifted his other ankle to the opposite knee, still smiling the entire time. "Kat, what were you thinking?"

"That I needed to get my family off my back," I said coldly. "That's what I was thinking."

"But you could have just been with me," he reasoned. "Wouldn't that make more sense than hiring some guy to be your boyfriend?"

"No, actually. Because you're a creep."

His eyes widened to orbs. I'd never said anything so cold to him and he didn't know how to process it.

"Cato was hired to be my boyfriend—in the beginning. But our relationship is different now. I truly care about him, and we have something really great. He's the first man I can see myself moving on with. Maybe I was paying for his time in the beginning, but now I'm not."

He nodded his head slowly. "And you expect me to believe that?"

"I don't care what you believe," I hissed. "Now get out of my office. I refuse to entertain a weasel when I have a million things to do."

"A weasel?" he asked coldly.

"Perfect description, isn't it?"

That annoying smile finally dropped from his face. "I wouldn't insult me if I were you."

"I'll do whatever I wish." I kept my hands on the desk so I wouldn't attack him.

He stared at me for a long time, his blue eyes darkening and becoming two lumps of coal. The muscles of his face remained perfectly still. It seemed like I was staring at a lifeless doll, but there was slight movement in his eyes. The silence weighed heavily in the room, and I didn't know what to expect next. Joey clearly had something on his mind, and judging the way he spoke, he'd rehearsed several times. "This is what's going to happen." His voice was low, like he feared someone would overhear. "You're going to end your little arrangement with Cato and you're going to date me—really date me."

How was I blind to Joey for so long? He was borderline crazy. "No."

"Yes." His eyes held his command.

I ground my teeth together. "I said no."

"If you continue to say no, I'll tell everyone what Cato does for a living. And I'll mention that you hired him to play a part. Not only will people think less of you and look down on you, but you'll be a joke to our society. No one will respect you, and more importantly, they'll pity you. You'll disgrace your parents, and they'll only smother you more." That smile returned to his lips, evil and full of malcontent. "You have no other choice but to get rid of Cato and give me a chance."

"No other choice?" I asked coldly. "I think otherwise."

"Oh really?" Judging his tone, he didn't believe me at all. "You think I'm bluffing?"

It took a lot to make me angry. After losing my husband in such a brutal way it made every other problem pale in comparison. I really understood pain and the depression that came along with it. Everything else was irrelevant.

But Joey was pissing me the fuck off.

I slowly rose to a stand, giving him the darkest look of menace I could muster. It easily stretched across my face, making my eyes burn with their own furnace. "If you have to resort to such measures just to land a girl, then I feel sorry for you. Tell everyone the truth, I really don't give a damn. I would much rather suffer that humiliation than ever be stuck on a date with a weasel like you."

His eyes burned in offense and his jaw was clenched tightly.

"Now get the hell out of my office."

***

I called Cato a few times but he didn't answer. I left him a voicemail the second I got off work, and after running a few errands before heading to my apartment, he still hadn't returned my call.

When hours passed, I started to get worried. He always took my calls. I couldn't recall a time when he didn't answer by the second ring. I called him again, needing to hear his voice.

"What?" Spikes of ice came through the phone and penetrated me. There was so much annoyance and irritation in his voice I thought I was speaking to someone I didn't know.

"Cato?"

"Who else would it be?" he snapped. "And why are you blowing up my phone? I'll call you back if and when I feel like it."

I stood in my kitchen and stared at the ground. The hostility burning through the receiver was terrifying. "Why are you so upset?"

"Maybe it's because I'm talking to you." He hung up.

I heard the line go dead. The phone was still held to my ear because I didn't know what else to do. Cato and I were fine yesterday. We had a great time and then we fooled around and played with our chemistry.

So what was his deal? I called him back.

"Fuck, you're annoying."

He'd never been so rude to me. Even when we first met it wasn't this bad. "Why are you being an asshole?"

"I'm being an asshole?" he asked incredulously. "You're the one being a bitch."

My heart sunk into my stomach. Did he really just call me that? "Why are you so pissed off? What the hell did I do?"

"The real question is, why do you care that I'm pissed off? I'm just some guy you fuck around with then throw outside like a damn dog. My feelings mean nothing to you. Never have and never will."

"I didn't throw you out like a dog. I was tired and needed to sleep."

"And why couldn't you sleep with me?" he demanded.

I didn't have a real answer. "I don't know...I just wasn't thinking about it."

Cato was quiet for a long time. But when he spoke again, his voice possessed more anger. "I told you I was looking for something more with you. I don't want to be used and tossed aside like garbage. You disrespected me and treated me like all the other guys you fuck and forget about. Just like the rest of them, you don't even remember what the fuck I look like. So, go pick up a different guy tonight. I'm no longer interested." He hung up.

I listened to the line go dead again.

***

Cato refused to take my calls. It always went to voicemail. I refused to leave a message because I assumed he wouldn't listen to it anyway.

When I asked him to leave my apartment, it wasn't because he didn't mean anything to me. It was just a habit. I felt terrible for giving him the wrong impression, for letting him think he was just a meaningless relationship. That wasn't true at all.

But he wouldn't let me apologize.

I didn't know where he lived and I wasn't sure how I would track him down. There was only one place I could go. And that was Beautiful Entourage.

When I approached Danielle's desk, she looked up at me with irritation. "How can I help you?"

"I was wondering if Cato was here...?" I looked around, hoping there was an office where he worked.

"He's not." She peeled a banana and ate it while she looked at her computer.

"Well, can you tell me where I can find him?" I asked hopefully.

"You have his number, don't you?" She refused to face me.

"Well, yeah. But I wanted to stop by his apartment and surprise him. Can you tell me where he lives?"

Danielle turned her brown eyes on me, and they were colder than the ice burg the Titanic crashed into. She slowly rose to her feet, her shoulders squared and her claws out and ready for a fight. "You hurt Cato." She stared into my eyes as she paused. "So you hurt me. I suggest you leave him alone and walk out now. Otherwise, I will stab you in the eye with a pen."

I didn't call her bluff. Wordlessly, I walked out and wondered what I would do next.

***

I worked from home for the next few days. I was too depressed to head to my office, and I feared Joey would make another appearance. Since I was so angry over Joey, I didn't trust myself not to stab in the balls with the heel of my stiletto and make him permanently infertile.

I called Cato throughout the day, hoping he would answer. Of course, he never did. Desperate to communicate with him, I started to leave voicemails. "Please call me back...I'm sorry." I hung up then waited for my phone to ring. It never did.

More hours passed and I tried to brainstorm a way of speaking to Cato. I needed to apologize and make him understand that he really meant something to me, that my behavior didn't represent the way I felt.

Since I was desperate, I did something extremely unethical. I left another voicemail and lied out of my ass.

"Cato, Joey is here and he won't leave me alone. He picked my lock and now I'm hiding in the bathroom. He's drunk and I'm scared..." I hung up and swallowed the lump in my throat.

I was a terrible person.

***

Cato practically broke the door off the hinges. It flew open so fast it slammed into the opposite wall and made a noticeable dent. His arms were stiff by his sides and he scanned the room for danger. The wicked gleam of violence was in his eyes, and he looked like he wanted to destroy someone.

His eyes eventually moved to my face. "Are you okay?" I was sitting at the kitchen table, so he kneeled down and examined me.

"I'm fine."

"Where is he?" He stood up again, looking around like Joey might pop out of the shadows.

I knew Cato was going to be pissed after I told him the truth. I closed the front door and pressed my back to it so he couldn't get out, unless he picked me up and moved me.

Cato turned to me and watched me with intelligent eyes. "Where is he?"

"He's not here..."

"He already left?" he asked. "I'll hunt him down. He better hope he's on an airplane because that's the only way I can't reach him."

I was about to be the recipient of those angry eyes and I didn't want to be. "He was never here, Cato. I made that up so you would come over." I cringed as his face contorted in a strong look of hate.

He took a few steps toward me, his powerful arms hanging by his sides. His strong body was formidable and I hoped I wouldn't be his next punching bag. He looked mad enough to rip me apart. "What the fuck did you just say?"

"I wanted to apologize...in person." I continued to block the door so he couldn't get out.

"You lied to me." It wasn't a question or a statement.

"I know...I was desperate. I wanted you to know I was sorry. When I didn't ask you to stay over that night, it wasn't personal. I just wasn't thinking. I've never had a guy stay over, and it's just a habit. You aren't meaningless to me and I'm sorry for making you think that."

Cato was still just as angry as before. "You kicked me out, Kat."

"No, I didn't. And I assumed you wanted to leave. We both had work the next day."

"What the fuck does that matter?" He stepped closer to me. "You would have slept with me then kicked me out before the following morning. Good thing I didn't let that happen."

"It's not like that," I argued. "Honestly. This is knew for me, and I asked you to be patient."

"I am being patient," he snarled. "But patience has nothing to do with this. You used me then cast me aside."

"No, I didn't," I argued. "Not at all."

He shook his head. "Just like last time..."

"Sorry?" I asked, unsure what he said.

"Nothing," he muttered. "Now get out of my way."

"No…not until we work this out."

His eyes darkened. "Move out of the way or I'll pick you up and move you."

I flattened my back against the door. "Let me prove it to you. Spend the night tonight."

"No," he hissed. "It doesn't mean anything when you're only doing it because I'm pissed off."

"That's not the only reason why I'm doing it, Cato," I said. "I really like you and I don't want to lose you."

"You already lost me, sweetheart.' His voice was full of condescension.

"Don't say that…" I felt my heart kick into overdrive. "This isn't worth breaking up over. Why are you jumping the gun?"

"Because I'm tired of you doing this to me."

"What?" I asked. "When have I done it before?"

He ignored my question. "You'll never change. I'll always be hung up on you, and you'll always be indifferent to me. If all you want is a meaningless fuck and someone to waste time with, then just admit it. Don't drag my heart through the mud."

"That isn't what I want!"

"That's how you treat me."

He wasn't making any sense. What was I missing? "Cato, please explain this to me. I don't understand."

"You don't understand how to treat a guy you're seeing with respect?" he demanded. "You really are a piece of work…" He marched toward the door and tried to get around me.

I tried to push him back and keep him on this side of the door. "Don't leave."

"I didn't want to leave—last week. But now I do." He grabbed my wrist and tried to yank me.

I pulled back. "No. I'm not letting you leave."

He ground his teeth as he stared me down. "Move. Or I'll throw you."

When he picked me up, I wouldn't be able to block the door anymore. He was twice my size and height. I had no chance. Instead, I went for the next alternative. I jumped into his arms and wrapped my legs around his waist.

Automatically, Cato caught me.

"Don't go." I looked down into his face with desperation in my eyes. "I'm sorry, okay?"

He wouldn't look at me. But he didn't throw me off either. "I know what this is about. If it'll get rid of you, fine."

What was he talking about?

Cato carried me to my bedroom then threw me on the bed. He started pulling my clothes off and his own.

This didn't feel like a make up session. It felt different, cold and detached.

"You want me to fuck you?" He got his boxers off then leaned over me. Then he opened my nightstand and grabbed a condom like he already knew they were there. He rolled it on.

"What the hell are you doing?" I put my hand against his chest.

"Let's just get this over with. You want me to stick it to you and never talk to you again. Well, you're getting your wish. I'll fuck you like you don't mean anything and then you can just leave me the hell alone. You win, Kat. I'm not sure why I thought I ever could." He leaned over me and separated my thighs with his. Then his tip pressed against my entrance.

"Stop!" I pushed his massive chest but nothing happened.

"Don't act like you don't want it."

I didn't like this at all. "Cato, stop. Now."

He froze while on top of me then gave me a dark look. Then he got off of me. Without taking the condom off, he put his clothes back on. He didn't look at me as he did it. "Joey seems like a guy who couldn't care less if you actually care about him at all. He's perfect for you." He left my bedroom.

"Cato!" I had my chest covered.

He opened the front door then slammed it.

***

I went to the bar Cato frequented in the hope I might see him. I searched the booths, feeling out of place for walking around alone. After taking a quick scan, I didn't see him.

"You look lost." A guy leaned against the table I was standing next to.

With one look, I recognized him. "Jett?"

"Hey." He raised his glass to me then took a drink. "On the prowl again, huh?"

So, Cato told him he we were done. "I'm looking for Cato."

"Why?" he asked.

"I need to talk to him. Please help me, Jett."

That smug smile left his face and he seemed uncomfortable. "I can't help you. Sorry."

"Don't be like that."

He took another drink before he set his beer down. "I pick on Cato a lot because I think he's an asshole, but in reality, he's one of my boys and I have his back forever, whether it's against bros or...the other one."

"It's a misunderstanding."

He shrugged. "Maybe it is. Maybe it isn't. All I know is, Cato has never been so hung up on a girl before. Now that he is, you keep hurting him left and right. I think he's finally given up on the possibility of you two being together. Frankly, he should."

"I don't hurt him left and right," I argued. "Where are you getting that from?"

He shrugged and took another drink.

"Give me his address."

"You're not really in the position to make demands."

"What do you want?" I opened my purse and pulled out my emergency funds. It was two hundred bucks. "Will this get you talking?"

He pushed my hand away. "I'm not for sale, sweetheart."

"Then please help me."

"I'm on Cato's side. It doesn't matter how pretty you are. Those charms won't work on me."

"You should help me since you're on Cato's side. I can't lose him. I love—" I stopped when I realized what I was going to say.

Jett's eyes were wide and he continued to watch me.

Did I just say that? Was that how I really felt? Was it too soon to feel that way? I'd only known Cato for three months. Wasn't it a little early for those feelings? And what about Ethan? Could I really love another man?

Jett continued to stare at me.

Was I actually pushing Cato away subconsciously because I was aware of this? Maybe I was doing this on purpose? I wasn't sure. But it scared me either way. Terrified me, actually. It was one thing to date someone new but another to love them altogether. How would Ethan feel about it? "I...I have to go." I grabbed my purse and ran through the doors like someone was chasing me.

***

Days passed and I didn't bother calling Cato. I just wanted to be alone after I blurted out those words. I was still processing them, trying to understand exactly how and when it happened.

Sometimes I felt like I already knew Cato. I recognized his body language, the way he held himself and moved. His kiss was familiar, like I already felt it once before. Perhaps it felt familiar because it felt right. Instead of bringing me closer to him, it pushed me away.

I wish I didn't have to act like this. I wish I didn't have any baggage like normal people. I wish I could stop living in my own world and join the rest of society.

I wish I could have Cato.

But I was scared. How could this work? Would I really let him in and let Ethan go? It was hard to marry someone and assume they would be by your side forever and then have them savagely taken away from you. How did you go on after that?

But I knew I needed to keep moving forward. And the fact I pretty much already moved on with Cato was terrifying. Even if I felt that way and wanted Cato, there was no way to get him back. He seemed set in his decision. He despised me just like he used to.

I was sitting in the living room when there was a knock on the door. The only person who would visit me unannounced was Joey, and he was the last person I wanted to see right now. Just thinking about him pissed me off.

I grabbed a frying pan before I answered the door, prepared to smack him hard in the face if I needed to. Maybe he needed a wake up call. I'd gladly oblige.

But Joey wasn't at the door. It was Cato.

He was leaning against the doorframe with his arms across his chest. He didn't look at me. His eyes searched the hallway like he expected to see someone he knew. He crossed one ankle, wearing jeans and a t-shirt. His hair was a little messy but not in a bad way. And his body looked nice in his clothes.

I lowered the frying pan so he wouldn't assume I planned to smack him. "Hi."

"Hey." He ran his fingers through his hair then stared at the ground.

Silence stretched—awkward silence.

"Do you want to come in?" I asked quietly.

"No."

"Okay..." I kept my stance. I hoped he came over here with the intention of working out our relationship. I didn't want us to end over a misunderstanding. I didn't want Cato to think he meant nothing to me.

"What's with the frying pan?" He didn't look directly at me so I wasn't sure how he spotted it.

"I thought you might be...someone else." I set the pan on the nearby table.

"Who?" he asked.

"Joey."

He finally faced me. "Is he bothering you? Or are you crying wolf right now?"

I deserved that. My cheeks tinted anyway. "Not exactly...he's just being a jackass."

"Tell me." His arms were still crossed over his chest but his shoulders were tense.

I shook my head in annoyance. "He found out you were a professional escort and he threatened to blackmail me and tell my entire family I was so pathetic that I hired you to pose as my boyfriend."

"In order to get you to do what?"

He already knew the answer. "Date him."

He silently asked me what my response was.

"I told him to go fuck himself. I don't care if he tells my family."

Approval moved into his eyes. "I'll take care of him for you."

"Don't do anything," I said immediately. "He's been working in business for years, so he knows the laws and the courts well. If he really wanted to make your life miserable with a lawsuit he could."

"You think I care?" he hissed. "No one threatens my girlfriend like that."

My heart swelled in joy and I felt the corners of my lips upturn in a smile. "Your girlfriend...?"

He looked into the hallway again.

I moved toward him to wrap my arms around him.

But he halted me in my tracks by extending his arm. "Whoa, hold on."

Defeated, I stepped back. We were so close but now we were far away again. "Cato, I said I was sorry. I meant it. I didn't kick you out because I saw our relationship as meaningless. Honestly, I just wasn't thinking. Please forgive me."

He crossed his arms again and remained quiet.

I stared at him, hoping he would accept my apology.

"I talked to Jett." He turned his eyes on me.

"I ran into him at a bar..."

He nodded. "He told me something interesting."

I crossed my arms over my chest because I suddenly felt vulnerable. "Yeah?"

"You said you loved me." He searched my face for a reaction. "Jett said it slipped out. Is that true?"

I didn't know how to respond. I may have felt that way but I wasn't ready to talk about it. "It might be..."

Cato shifted his weight but didn't come any closer. "Well, is it?"

I tucked a strand of hair behind my ear, feeling nervous. I was being put on the spot and I didn't like it. I was starting to sweat.

"Why won't you answer my question?"

"Just because I feel that way doesn't mean I'm ready to say it." My voice came out weak and quiet.

His eyes lightened. "But you do...feel that way?"

I nodded slightly.

"That was the only reason I came back here. I hope you realize that."

"Then I'm glad I said it."

He relaxed his body then wrapped one arm around my waist. He pulled me to him and pressed his forehead against mine. He held me outside the apartment, his chest pressed against mine. He gave me a gentle kiss on the neck, soft enough to be from the touch of a butterfly.

I closed my eyes and enjoyed it.

"You really hurt me." He brought his face back to mine.

"I know. I'm sorry."

"Don't hurt me again. I couldn't handle it a third time."

"When was the second?" I asked.

"Actually, the first."

What?

He led me inside the apartment then closed the door. Now we weren't out in public for everyone to see. His hands moved to my hips then he kissed the corner of my mouth.

"I'm sorry."

"It's okay," he whispered.

"You want to spend the night?" I hoped the gesture wouldn't come off fake. It wasn't just a false act to keep him around.

"Yeah?" His lips curled into a smile I'd come to love.

"Yeah."

"I'd love to. As long as you'll be there when I wake up."

"Of course I will."

He grabbed my chin and forced my look on him. "Promise?"

He'd never made me promise anything before. It must be really important to him. "I promise."

***

I wore my t-shirt and panties while he slept in the nude. He faced me in bed, his arm around my waist with his forehead close to mine. I hadn't had a guy sleep over in years. The last man I slept with all night was Ethan.

"I'm surprised it bothered you so much," I whispered. "You strike me as the kind of guy who lives for one-night stands."

"I was. But we both know I'm different with you."

"I've never seen you so upset."

"You drive me crazy." He ran his hand up and down my hip, trailing his fingers across the skin.

"Crazy?" I asked, slightly playful.

"Insane." He rubbed his nose against mine. "You like bowling?"

The question was random. "Why do you ask…?"

"You want to go bowling tomorrow?"

"Why do you always want to do an activity?" I asked with a laugh.

"Because they're fun. And I have fun doing them with you."

"Well, I'm not the best bowler," I said. "I've only done it a handful of times."

"I didn't ask if you were the best bowler. I just asked if you wanted to bowl with me."

"As long as you don't tease me."

He released a faint chuckle. "That's impossible. I'll always tease you."

"Good to know..."

He pulled me closer into him. "It's a good thing. I only tease the people in my inner circle. And you're officially in it."

"I am?" I felt his hard chest.

"Yep." He looked into my eyes. "But you already knew that."

***

"Is this okay?" I wore jeans and a Rolling Stones t-shirt.

He looked me up and down. "More than okay. You have great taste in music."

"You like them?"

"They are on my top five." He grabbed my hand and we left the apartment.

"Who else is on the list?"

"The Doors, Jimi Hendrix, Alice in Chains, and Black Sabbath."

"Good lineup."

He rubbed his nose against mine. "I knew you were special. I just knew it."

We entered the bowling alley then grabbed our gear.

"A few friends are joining us. Is that cool?"

I thought it was odd that he didn't mention this until we arrived. And I already met his friends countless times. What was the need for secrecy? "Just the guys?"

"Actually, it's an old friend with his wife and daughter."

An old friend? "Like, they're a family?"

"Yeah, but they are good friends."

"Why would you invite them to bowl with us?"

He shrugged. "I thought it would be fun. Are you really that averse to getting to know new people?"

"No," I said immediately. "I just find it odd you didn't mention people would be joining us."

"Why?" He put his arm around me. "You wanted me all to yourself, huh?" That cocky look was back on his face. I missed it so I didn't make a smartass comment back.

"Yeah...I guess so."

"Not surprised."

We reached our lane and Cato's friends were already there. A man who looked middle age but young was tying his shoes. He had thick arms like Cato, and when he stood up he was just as tall.

"Hey, Cato." He clapped him on the shoulder.

"Hey." Cato acknowledged him back. "This is my girlfriend, Katarina."

I shook his hand. "Call me Kat. It's nice to meet you."

Dark Escort

He smiled while he took me in, his eyes glowing. "Call me Tom. It's lovely to meet you."

His wife came next. "Wow, you're so pretty," she blurted.

I blushed but chuckled. "Thanks. I'm Kat."

"It's great to meet you." Instead of shaking my hand, she hugged me.

I was caught off guard by the affection but I returned the embrace. "You too."

"I'm Lisa." She pulled away and smiled. "And we're excited you're both here."

A girl a few years younger than me joined us. "Hey, Cato." She didn't hug him, just acknowledged him with a nod.

"Hey, Amber." He nudged her in the side then introduced me. "This is Kat."

Amber shook my hand quickly. "You sure you want to be with this loser?"

I chuckled. "I think he's a winner."

She rolled her eyes. "Wait until you get to know him better."

"Are we going to talk shit all day or are we going to bowl?" Cato put on his shoes then set up the bowling schedule.

"Told you." Amber flipped her hair then sat down.

Lisa sat in the chair beside me. She had bright blonde hair, and she had a little extra weight along her hips and thighs. But she was fairly thin. "So, you work for a winery?"

"Yeah, my family owns it. And I drink it."

219

She laughed at my joke. "I love wine."

"I'll get you a bottle," I offered. "They're just lying around the office. And if I don't hand them out, I'll end up drinking them."

"First world problems," she said with a laugh.

"I know, right?"

Cato bowled first and rolled a spare. "That's how it's done, boys and girls."

"Shut up, Cato," Tom said. He stood up and bowled next.

I turned to Lisa. "How do you guys know Cato?"

"Uh..." She shot him a look before she turned back to me. "Tom was his professor in college. They've been close ever since."

"Oh, that's really cool."

"He's like a son to us. We enjoy spending time with him."

"Cato is a pretty terrific guy," I blurted. "He wasn't what he seemed in the beginning but he turned out to be a lot more than I ever could have imagined."

She smiled while she listened to me. "He's a catch— if you can get him to be serious."

I chuckled. "True."

"Cato mentioned you're a widow..."

"Oh yeah." I shrugged. "He passed away five years ago in the military."

"I'm so sorry, dear." She patted my back. "That must have been hard."

"It was," I said. "I've been alone ever since. Well, until Cato."

"You deserve another chance at love," she said. "And I think Cato will be the perfect guy for that."

"I'm starting to think that too."

Amber rolled, and she surprised all of us by rolling a strike. She gave Cato the bird. "Now that's how it's done, asshole."

One side of Cato's mouth lifted into a half smirk. "Brat..."

It was my turn so I picked up the ball and put my fingers inside it. I got ready to roll it then swung my arm back.

"Baby, stop."

I looked over my shoulder. "What?"

"You're doing it all wrong." He tried not to laugh. "You're going to dislocate your shoulder at that rate."

"I told you I wasn't a good bowler."

"But you didn't tell me you were totally clueless."

I glared at him. "Are you going to help me or are you going to continue being a jackass?"

That cocky smirk came back. "I'll show you." He helped me with my form and stood behind me as he taught me how to aim and roll. "There. Now you won't break your arm." He smacked my ass playfully. "Now do it, milkshake."

I rolled the ball, and to my astonishment, I rolled a strike. I jumped in the air and threw my arms out. "Oh yeah! Look! I did it!" I turned to Cato and watched him smile. "I rolled a strike."

"I know. I saw."

I jumped into his arms and wrapped my legs around his waist. "Look who's got competition now?"

He gripped my ass and kissed me. "I've always wanted a woman to kick my ass." He kissed me as he carried me back to the chairs.

"Well, you got it." I forgot about his friends.

"Get a room," Amber said as she rolled her eyes.

"This is a room." Cato sat down with me on his lap.

"Gross," she whispered.

Cato's turn came up again and he left me alone in the seat.

"You guys are cute together," Lisa said. She couldn't stop smiling. It was like her face was permanently stuck that way.

"Thanks…"

"Tom and I wondered if he would ever settle down. I'm glad he has."

I was surprised his old professor cared about his personal life. Maybe they were closer than he let on.

We continued the game until we finished. Cato came in first and I came in a close second.

"You shouldn't have shown me your secrets," I said. "Now you created a monster."

He put his arm around my shoulder as we walked out to the parking lot. "My lady is my equal. We're a team."

"Last time I checked, you weren't a feminist."

"I'm half feminist, half chivalrous."

"I guess I can settle for that."

When we reached the cars, we said our goodbyes.

Tom hugged me. "We should do this again. But you can be on my team."

I chuckled. "That would be fun. I'm in."

Amber waved at me quickly before she got inside the car.

Cato hugged Lisa for a long time.

"I love her," Lisa whispered.

"I knew you would," he whispered back.

That was flattering.

Lisa then hugged me and held me tightly. "Please come over for dinner sometime."

"Sure," I said automatically. "I'd love to."

She gave me another hug before she got into the car with her husband.

Cato pulled me into him as we headed to his car.

"You guys are really close, huh?"

He opened the passenger door and let me get inside before he shut the door. After he came around the car, he got into the driver's seat. "Yeah, I'd say so."

"You must have been an astute student."

"Something like that." He started the car and got the radio on.

"If I didn't know they were just friends, I would assume they were your family or something." I looked out the window and listened to the radio.

"Well..."

I turned back to him, wondering what he meant. "Well, what?"

"I lied before..."

Panic came into my veins. "Lied? What do you mean?"

"They are my parents." His lips upturned in an involuntary smile. He tried to fight it but he was failing.

"What?" My voice came out as a shriek. I thought of the way I jumped into his arms and wrapped my arms around his neck. I thought of the way I kissed him and sat in his lap. Then I told his mom about how much I liked him...oh god. "I can't believe you did that!"

He laughed. "I knew you would freak out if I told you they were my parents. I feared you wouldn't agree to go at all."

"And that's my own right!" I kept yelling and couldn't stop myself.

He wouldn't stop smiling. "They loved you. Like, really loved you. So, calm down."

"But I wasn't ready to meet your parents," I hissed.

"And you never would have been," he argued. "I gave you a little push and I'm glad I did. If you really gave this a chance we could have something pretty fucking amazing. You already feel something strong for me and you want to be with me, but you keep me at a distance. You need to stop and let me in."

I turned back to the window. "It's complicated..."

"I understand the situation. I really do. But it's time to let it go."

I knew what he meant. I knew whom he was referring to.

"You aren't doing anything wrong," he said gently. "We're great together. Let me in—for real. Otherwise, this relationship won't survive." He didn't drive away. The car was on but it was in park. The music played in the background. "Come on, Katarina."

I didn't face him because I couldn't do it. "Take me home."

He sighed from his side of the car. "Don't shut me out."

"Just take me home."

He didn't take off. Instead, he sat there for several minutes, waiting for me to say something. When I didn't, he finally put the car in drive. "I'll put up with a lot, Katarina. But I won't put up with it for long."

***

The only sign of life at the cemetery were the birds. They emitted their high-pitched cries as they bounced around the branches. They called out to one another and sang their song.

I reached the grave where my husband lay. I stared down at it, seeing his name and years lived. The symbol of the armed forces was engraved in the stone. I stood there for a long time as I stared at the tombstone, being silent in his honor.

My favorite flowers were lilies, so I placed them on his grave. He used to bring them home every time he returned from being on leave. It was a tradition that didn't last long.

The breeze moved through my hair as I stood there. It was hard to believe he'd been gone for five years. It seemed like I just lost him yesterday. But it also seemed like an eternity since I last felt him.

I came to see him fairly often. It didn't comfort me but it didn't make me break down in tears either. It was the only connection I had to him on this side of life.

I stood there for a long time, wondering if he knew I was there. Sometimes I felt his spirit move through me, touching my hair or lightly grazing my cheek. It could be just a trick of my imagination but I pretended it wasn't.

The sun was hot on my skin, making me warm. There were no nearby trees to provide adequate shade. But I would stand there until I was ready to leave. Could I really love another man, even marry him someday? Wasn't Ethan my only chance of love? Wasn't that how it was supposed to be? He told me to move on if he ever died, but did he really mean that?

"I've always loved that dress."

I looked up to see Ethan leaning against his tombstone. I knew it was a projection of my mind, a daydream that wasn't real. But that didn't mean I didn't enjoy it. His jaw was scruffy from not shaving, which wasn't surprising. He always hated shaving. And he wore his typical gray t-shirt and dark jeans. "Why do you think I wore it?"

He gave me a smile that showed all of his teeth. He was too handsome for his own good, and that always made him cocky. He'd been cocky since the day we met at that bar. "With legs like that you need to show them off."

I stared at him and wished I could touch him. Even now, I still missed that embrace.

His smile faded away. "Sugar, don't be sad."

He always called me sugar. He was from the south, so I assumed that's where he got it from.

He moved away from the tombstone and came closer to me. "You know I love you. So seeing you like this, mourning for me still, breaks my heart. It's okay to move on."

"It is?" I felt my eyes burn but my tears didn't fall.

"It is." His eyes narrowed on my face, watching the moisture build up in my eyes. "We only had a year together but it was a pretty terrific year. And now I'm gone. You think I want you to be alone forever?"

I shook my head slightly, unable to speak.

"I want you to be happy. Please be happy."

"Really?"

"Of course. I want you to have lots of babies. So many babies you don't even know what to do with them." His smile had returned.

I released a faint chuckle. "Lots of babies, huh?"

"Yeah, and with a good guy. I like Cato."

"You do?"

"I can tell he loves you. And that's really all I care about."

"He does, doesn't it?" I thought I noticed it but would never admit it.

"Stop holding onto me. You aren't betraying me or what we had. Let me go."

"I can never let you go," I said quietly.

"I'm not asking you to forget about me," he said. "But I'm asking you to move on with your life. Who you love now doesn't affect what we had. But what we had shouldn't affect what you have now."

I knew he was right. "Okay..."

"Okay?" He smiled wide. "You're going to finally get off your high horse and stop dragging this guy through the mud? That guy has jumped some serious hoops for you. Give him a real chance."

"He deserves it."

"He deserves it because you love him."

I didn't deny it. And for the first time, I didn't feel bad about that.

Ethan looked at me with those scorching blue eyes. "Now go live what's left of your life. You've already wasted five years of it."

I nodded.

"I'll always love you, Sugar. Never forget that."

"I love you too," I whispered.

"Now go love him with everything you have, have a great life together, and make those babies."

I chuckled even though my throat hurt. "I can do that."

"Good. Don't let me down."

"Never."

He gave me one final look before he disappeared.

The sound of the birds came back to my ears. The rays of the sun pounded into my skin. And the breeze moved through my strands of hair. Somehow, I knew Ethan wanted me to move on.

I just knew.

***

I asked Cato to come over. He didn't question my odd request or the weird way I asked it. He just obeyed without question.

He walked inside and gave me a quick kiss on the lips. Judging his stiffness he was still upset with me over the bowling fiasco. I pushed him away when he tried to open up to me. He was integrating me with his family, trying to get me to loosen up and start over. Instead of appreciating that, I pushed him away.

He put his hands in his pockets then looked around my apartment. "So, what's up?" There was a guarded expression in his eyes, like he feared what I might say or do.

"I wanted to talk to you about something..." I knew I was going to sound like a crazy person when I said it.

He shifted his weight and suddenly became defensive. "If you're going to break up with me because you aren't ready for a serious relationship, I don't accept that. I will never accept that. You're wasting your time."

His words surprised me. There were times when it seemed like he didn't want to put up with me. But he always came back, ready for a fight. "No, that's not what I was going to say."

"That's a surprise." He didn't hide his sarcasm.

I fidgeted with my hands, unsure how to verbalize my thoughts. Cato might think I was weird or insane but he might not. "I went to the cemetery yesterday and I talked to Ethan..."

His aggression died away and he watched me with passive eyes.

"He wants me to move on and he wants me to be happy. As long as you're a good guy, that's all that matters. Being alone isn't what he wants. He wants me to have babies and...live my life without mourning him forever."

Cato didn't make fun of me or call me crazy. He just listened.

"And he knows I love you."

He still didn't say anything.

"So, I wanted you to know that I'm ready to make this relationship work. I'm ready to give everything I have and let you in. That is...if you still want to put up with me."

His eyes softened and a slight smile stretched his lips. "I'll always put up with you, no matter how annoying you are." He approached me then placed his hands on my hips. He looked into my face then rubbed his nose against mine.

An invisible weight left my shoulders, and I finally let my walls come down. The guilt was gone and I let Cato look at me for the first time, seeing all of me. I had nothing to hide and I wasn't putting distance between us.

"You still want to know why I disliked you so much?"

It was such a random thing to say. But I knew it must have some relevance. "Yes."

"Then let me show you."

Cato

Secretly, I feared Katarina would never truly let me in. I thought it would be an uphill battle, constant and difficult to defeat. Every time we got closer to the top, we would roll and fall back down to the bottom. Even when this was a serious possibility, I still tried to make it work.

Because I wanted her.

Now that she met my family and she said she was ready to be serious with me, I thought it was best if I told her the truth. It might bring us closer together. Or it might push her away. But either way, I had to tell her. It was a secret I couldn't keep for the rest of my life.

I picked her up at eleven thirty in the evening, which was much later than we would normally go out. Around that time, we were normally getting home from a restaurant and preparing for bed. But that was the time it had to be.

She opened the door wearing jeans and a jacket. "I still don't understand why you have to explain this to me so late at night."

"You'll see."

"Okay." She yawned.

"Is it past the baby's bedtime?" I teased.

She smiled then smacked my arm. "Don't be a jerk."

I pushed her against the door then gave her a hard kiss. "I'll be a jerk when I feel like it. And we both know you love it." I gave her another kiss then dragged her from the apartment.

"I love it sometimes…"

Hand-in-hand we left her apartment and headed to Times Square. The streets were slightly less crowded than normal since everyone was home by now. Having some privacy would be nice.

We crossed the street then reached the sidewalk on the corner. On New Year's Eve we were in the street, but due to the constant traffic I couldn't stand on the pavement with her. The corner would have to do.

I stopped and stared at her expression.

She looked around, confused. "Um…okay."

"This is where they drop the ball every year."

"I know." She crossed her arms over her chest and looked up into the sky, where they would normally have it hanging. "So?" She turned back to me.

For better or for worse, here goes nothing. "I wanted to tell you something but I had to do it here."

She patiently waited for me to elaborate.

"My life before you was filled with girls whose names I'll never remember, parties where I was so drunk I didn't even know who I went home with, and threesomes and foursomes. My life was awesome and I never wanted to change it. A few of my friends settled down but I thought they were making the biggest mistake of their lives. Little did I know living without you was the biggest mistake of mine."

Her eyes softened while she listened to me.

"You already know how I feel about you even though I've never actually said it. But that's how you know it's real. I don't need to say the words to prove anything. My actions speak louder. I've worked hard to make this relationship work because you're the prize I was desperate to have. So…I wanted to say those words now." I swallowed the lump in my throat because I was nervous. I'd never done this before. I'd never felt this way for anyone in my life. "I love you, Katarina."

Her eyes watered while a weak smile formed on her lips. She seemed moved beyond words and understanding. She blinked her eyes several times to dispel the moisture.

My heart raced as I waited for her to say it back. She never said it to me directly before, and I was eager to hear my words echoed back at me.

"I love you too."

My heart relaxed and I floated in the air. Knowing she felt the same way I did made all this effort worth it. I didn't understand why she was the one, but she was. It was an innate truth.

My watched beeped as midnight struck. "I remember what you were wearing the very first time I saw you. You wore a gray beanie to keep your head warm from the cold, and you wore a blood red jacket."

Her eyes dilated and her face turned pale.

"The first time we met wasn't in that coffee shop when you hired me. It was here, exactly two years ago. I spotted you in the crowd and thought you were cute as hell. I walked up to you and made my move to charm you. In the end, you charmed me when you told me your new year's resolution was to eat the different flavors of Oreos."

She covered her mouth as she gasped.

"Words were said, and we went back to my place and had the best sex I've ever had. I fell for you, even then. You were the first girl I met that I wanted to know more about. I didn't want it to be a one-night stand. I wanted so much more. But when I woke up, you were gone...I never even knew your name."

Her eyes were wide as everything came back to her. She looked at me with new eyes, seeing me in a different way.

I opened my wallet then pulled out the note she left. The fact I saved it at all told me she meant something to me, meant more than any girl ever would. I handed it to her.

She took it with a shaky hand then read it. "Happy New Year. Every time I eat a root beer flavored Oreo I'll think of you." She took a deep breath and read the note again. Her eyes scanned from left to right. "Oh my god..."

"I've pursued you so hard because...as crazy as this sounds...I think we're meant to be together. What are the odds of us meeting on New Year's Eve? Slim to none. Seven million people live in this city. But to meet again two years later...baffles me. I've never believed in fate or divine intervention but...I believe in whatever this is."

She felt the note in her fingers while she looked at me.

"I was rude to you because I was hurt you didn't remember me. You didn't recognize me at all. Not only did that hurt my ego and pride, but it also wounded me. That night meant something to me. And you just left the next morning without even telling me your name..."

She covered her face as the realization hit her. "That's why you were so upset when I didn't want to sleep with you...you thought I was leaving you again."

I nodded.

She looked down at the note again.

"It's been driving me crazy, Katarina. How could you not remember me?" Did I really want to know? There was no answer that she would give that would make me feel better. I wasn't memorable to her, plain and simple.

"I was drunk that night. And I have a poor memory when I'm drunk."

"You were?" I asked in surprise.

"Honestly, I didn't remember any of that until you got my memory going. I remember standing in Times Square and meeting you, and I vaguely remember the Oreos, but I don't remember sleeping with you at all. The only reason why I recognize this note is because it's in my handwriting and has the correct signature."

Now I felt a little better. She didn't remember me because I wasn't worth remembering. She was just out of her mind.

"I really wish I did remember...I might have stayed the following morning if I had. I find it hard to believe I would ever walk away from you."

I put my hands in my pockets and relived that night behind my eyes.

"Why did you wait so long to tell me?"

"I hoped you would remember me on your own. That was why I took you to the same convenient store and bought Oreos. That's why I kissed you against the side of the building. I thought it would come back to you. But when it was clear you wouldn't remember, I knew I had to tell you. You were the one that got away and then you came back into my life. That's why I don't care about your emotional issues. Because...I know you're meant for me."

There was a possibility that statement might offend her since she was already married. Chances are, she thought she was meant for him, not me. But I had to say it because it was how I really felt.

"I think you're right," she whispered.

I wasn't expecting her to say that.

"I loved my husband with everything I had. We were passionate and desperately in love. But I never thought he and I were meant to be together. I chose to love him because he was the man I wanted. What we had was beautiful, and just the fact I could possibly love another man besides him...tells me something. I could only feel that way if there was something special about him, something divine." She looked at me with those beautiful blue eyes I loved. They reflected the light from above, just like they did on that magical night.

The night deepened and all sound suddenly disappeared. It was just she and I, on the cliff face of a new beginning. It took me a long time to find her again, and I found her under the worst circumstances. But I did find her again. And it took even longer for her to find me.

But we made it.

"I wanted to tell you I loved you at the place where I actually knew I loved you. Hence, why we're here."

Her lips stretched into a smile. "That's one of the most romantic things I've ever heard."

I grabbed her hips and pulled her to me. My mind was in a different place, soaring over the clouds at the speed of light. A moment like this didn't happen for most people. But it happened for me. I wasn't looking for her when I found her. She stumbled into my life like a shooting star, making an appearance without knowing where she came from.

And now she was mine.

***

I took her back to my place for the first time—well, technically the second.

Katarina looked around as she entered. She took in the kitchen, living room, and dining room. There wasn't any recognition on her face, any familiarity. I was hoping she would remember it and I was disappointed when she didn't.

Reading my mind she turned to me. "You'll help me remember."

"I'm sure I will." I didn't bother turning on the lights because I knew what would happen between us. Neither one of us said it, but it was obvious in the way we behaved around one another.

Now that I knew she felt the way I did, I wasn't scared. She'd given herself to me in a different way. Our souls were already joined, had been joined on that night two years ago. Who she loved before I came along was irrelevant. I had skeletons in my closet from my past, and that didn't matter either.

I moved across the floor until I reached her, and I gripped her hips with my hands. With my forehead pressed to hers, I stripped her jacket off, wanting to see those gorgeous curves under the fabric.

I led her to my bedroom as we went, and my lips found hers in a heated embrace. Her hands dug into my hair, and she kissed me with more passion than she ever had before. Her walls were gone and she was letting me in for the first time, completely and utterly.

When we reached the foot of the bed, we continued to consume each other in desperation. Her hands moved to my shirt and yanked it off. Then she kissed my chest as she moved for my jeans.

My lips moved to her neck and I kissed her as she undressed me. Watching her tear my clothes off with desperation was exciting, and my cock was throbbing due to its hardness.

Katarina peeled my boxers away and let him hang out. Her lips found mine again and she gripped the shaft and started to massage him slowly. Fluid leaked from my tip, and she used it as lubricant to stroke me.

I wanted to come undone because of her obvious beauty and perfection. But she knew how to please a man right, and that was impossible to resist. I reached for her clothes and stripped her down to her panties. I played with the fabric for a while before I pulled them off, loving the feel of the lace on my fingertips. "You're just as beautiful as I remember." I picked her up then placed her on my bed.

She pulled me into her with enthusiasm and wrapped her long legs around my waist. Our bodies were pressed tightly together and our breathing was in sync. Her eyes burned in desire as she looked into my face. I couldn't wait to connect our bodies together, to make love for the first time. Last time I just fucked her. I didn't want that again. I opened my nightstand and grabbed a condom.

"No." She grabbed my wrist and stilled it. "I want to feel you."

And I definitely wanted to feel her. "I want kids someday but not now."

"I'm on the pill." Her eyes flashed with humor. "And I don't want anything to separate us."

The gesture wasn't lost on me. She wouldn't offer that unless she was in love with me. I tossed the condom aside then positioned myself to enter her. I'd never had sex without a condom, and all the guys said it was the most amazing thing in the world.

When I slid inside her, I knew what they meant. "Oh shit." I completely sheathed myself because she was so wet and slick. Then I took a deep breath and acclimated to the goodness between her legs.

"Cato...you feel so good." Her nails dug into me as she held on.

"There's no comparison," I said with a grunt. I didn't move inside her. Instead I looked down into her face then kissed her. I concentrated on the feel of our mouths moving together, trying to get her as aroused as possible. I knew I wouldn't last long, not when we were skin-to-skin like this.

She started to rock into me from below.

Goddammit, she felt good. I knew I needed to stop being a pussy and man up. My woman needed to be pleased. I moved one hand to her lower back and lifted her slightly, deepening the angle. Then I gave her all of me in long, even strokes.

"Oh..." Her head rolled back as she felt me hit her in the right spot.

I watched her enjoy me, loving the feel of me as I moved in and out. My breathing increased and I started to sweat. I couldn't stop thinking about how beautiful she was, how happy she made me. Our love didn't start out the right way but it ended the right way. And that was all that really mattered.

"Cato..." She gripped my shoulders so she could use her lower body to sheath me harder. "I love you."

Her words made my heart burst. "And I love you."

Katarina bit her lip as her face and chest flushed. Then her nails dug into me and she tightened around me. I felt her constrict my dick as she prepared for the bout of pleasure about to rock her. Then I felt her come all over my dick. It was the sexiest sensation I'd ever felt. "Yes…" Her nails slowly pulled out of my skin and she caught her breath.

I'd do a better job next time we made love but I couldn't hold on any longer. Watching her and feeling her hit her climax was enough to make me come undone. I pulled her further into me, getting prepared to come deep inside her. I'd never come directly inside a girl before. Now would be my first, and just the thought made me want to explode.

Katarina pulled her legs back, allowing me more room. She propped herself on her elbows while she looked at me. "Come inside me, Cato."

There was no fucking way I would last now. I pumped into her hard and fast then felt the burn deep in my body. It spread to every fiber and nerve and then exploded between my legs. It dragged on forever, lasting longer than I thought possible. I stayed inside her as my body adjusted to the after shocks of pleasure. I remained inside her, loving the way it felt.

Not wanting to be separated, I rolled to my side and kept her close to me. Her leg hooked around my waist and I stayed deep inside her. I was starting to soften but when I was ready for another go we would be prepared.

She ran her fingers through my hair while she stared at me.

I kept my eyes open even though I was exhausted.

Then she sat up. "Well, I'm going to go…"

What?

She smiled at the panicked look on my face. "Kidding."

I relaxed then nudged her playfully. "Brat."

"You know I would never leave you, Cato. Not again."

With those final words, I pulled her into me again and fell into a deep sleep.

***

Katarina stayed with me the entire week. After she got tired of going back and forth to her apartment for her clothes, make up, and hair supplies she brought a bag and left it at my house.

I was one happy man.

She slept with me every night, and when I woke up in the morning, she had breakfast ready with a fresh brewed coffee. The apartment was noticeably cleaner, and my towels were no longer on the floor of the bathroom. Fresh, clean ones were always hanging from the rack. And the apartment had a new scent to it.

Her scent.

I never had a girl stay with me before. I forgot about them as soon as I rolled the condom off my dick. Like she did to me, I kicked them out. I didn't do sleepovers. But Katarina was a nice addition to my life.

She was organizing her briefcase while sipping her coffee one morning. She was dressed for work, wearing a tight pencil skirt and a pink blouse. Heels were on her feet, and her hair was pulled back. She looked like a sexy CEO.

Katarina noticed me staring at her. "What?" She kept sorting through her papers.

"I think you're hot."

A slight smile crept into her lips. "Yeah?"

"Uh-huh."

"Well, thank you."

"A quickie before work?"

She smiled again. "I don't have time, Cato. And you know me. I always like seconds afterward."

I took a drink of my coffee. "Never forget."

She closed her briefcase then put it over one shoulder. "I'll see you when I get off work."

"Will you cook dinner for me?" That was another perk. A hot meal was on the table every night. All I had to do was help her clean up the dishes afterward. And I had leftovers throughout the day. It was a sweet deal.

"When have I ever let my man go hungry?"

"Never." I put my hands behind my head and leaned back.

She walked to me then gave me a quick kiss on the lips. "I'll see you later."

When she was about to pull away, I snatched her and pulled her onto my lap. My arm tightened around her so she couldn't get away. I kissed her hard, loosening her resolve to run away.

"I'm going to be late," she said as she continued to kiss me.

"So? You run the damn thing." I knocked my coffee cup and plate onto the floor. It crashed into several pieces when it hit the hard wood floor. I couldn't care less about my dishes and threw Katarina on the table. Her skirt was up, and my pants were down. Then I slipped inside her and gave her the quickest quickie she'd ever had in her life.

***

Troy mentioned Harper had an issue with him working as an escort. I understood the complication because our job was unusual. Honestly, who wanted their man touching other women?

But it didn't seem to be an issue with Katarina.

She never asked me about my work, and when I had to escort a client on a Friday or Saturday evening, she never got upset. She usually worked until I came home. Then we had our fun.

I assumed it was because she trusted me. I worked really hard to get Katarina into my life and to get her to trust me. It wouldn't make any sense for me to fall for someone else.

Our relationship had changed since that evening in Times Square. It was stronger and more passionate. She treated me like I was water, food, and air. She couldn't live without me, and if she had to, she didn't last very long.

It was exactly what I wanted. Having Katarina was like having a best friend you enjoyed having sex with. When I was finished and satisfied, I still wanted to be around her all the time. We could be lying on the TV watching a boring documentary but I didn't care. As long as I was with her, I was happy.

When she told me she talked to her husband and had some divine intervention, I didn't question it. And I didn't think she was crazy. When you lose someone, are they ever really gone? The important thing was, she had permission to be happy with me.

And now we were.

She used to get these random looks of sadness when we were together. Now when I thought about it I retrospect, I realized she was thinking about him. In what context, I wasn't sure. She either missed him or felt guilty for spending time with me. But she didn't make those faces anymore.

If Ethan ever did come up, it was in a good way. If something related to the military came up, she told me how many tours he did or how he enlisted. But when she talked about him, it was with a smile on her face. She felt comfortable talking about him to me, keeping him alive in a way, but she also got to keep me.

It worked.

The only bad thing about our relationship, which really had nothing to do with either of us, was our work schedules. She worked mornings and I worked nights. Sometimes we didn't see each other until I got off work. But I could tell she missed me by the way she enthusiastically greeted me.

My parents adored her. When I told them about her, my mom was about to have a heart attack. She thought I would never bring a girl around. There was even a point in time when she thought I was gay. I quickly corrected her and told her I was a hit it and quit it kind of guy.

She wasn't impressed by that.

But now my mom was over the moon. Katarina was clearly a good girl who was independent, smart, and beautiful. Dad liked her too, and they were eager for me to settle down and take a wife.

A wife would be nice.

Jett came over during the day since he had nothing to do before work that evening. We usually played video games together because I just got a new console. As soon as we walked inside he grabbed a beer then plopped down on the couch. But then his face changed. "What the hell is that smell?"

"What smell?" I sniffed the air. "I don't smell anything."

"It smells like..." He took another deep breath. "Like a summer meadow."

"Have you been to a summer meadow lately...?"

He glanced at the coffee table, which had two pink candles, and then turned to the other couch to see a pair of heels thrown on top. Katarina's things were scattered around everywhere. I'd gotten used to it so I didn't even notice. "Is she living here?"

"No...but pretty much." I smiled because I couldn't help it.

"So, are you guys serious now or is she still...you know?"

"We're great," I said. "I told her about New Year's Eve and then we had sex. It's been great ever since."

"And her husband?"

"She made her peace with it. She's ready to move on now."

He nodded. "Congratulations, man."

"Thanks."

"Good sex?"

"She's just as amazing as before."

"Sweet." He tapped his beer against mine. "What's next?"

"What do you mean?"

"You going to move in with her or something? Propose? Rhett shacked up with Aspen immediately, and Troy followed in his footsteps. Are you going to do the same?"

I never seriously considered it. I would love to live with her. That wasn't the issue. I just wasn't sure if she wanted to. If I asked, what if it backfired? We were doing really well. Doing too much could damage it. "I wouldn't mind living with her."

"Are you going to ask then?"

"I don't know…I'll feel her out."

He shook his head and mumbled. "Pussy."

"You're just jealous you're alone."

He laughed. "Believe me, I'm not. You should be jealous of me, man."

"I'm definitely not." I'd already had that lifestyle and it was pretty hollow and meaningless. When Jett found a girl he really liked he would see what I meant. Until then, he wouldn't understand.

A knock on the door broke our conversation.

"Hooker?" Jett asked with a grin.

"Maybe for you." I walked to the door then looked through the peephole. When I saw the person on the other side I wanted to break my door just so I could throw it at him. "Mother fucker."

"Who is it?" Jett asked.

"Someone that's about to die." I opened the door and came face-to-face with the man I despised most.

Joey.

"You have a death wish?" I demanded. I was already rolling up my sleeves with every intention of breaking every bone in his face.

He wore a somber look. He didn't rise to my challenge, throw a comment back, or even acted like he cared at all.

"You're going to make it that easy on me?" I asked.

Jett came up behind me. "Two on one. I like those odds."

Joey looked at him but didn't show any fear.

"What the fuck do you want, weasel?" I asked.

"Mercy." That was all he said.

"Mercy?" I asked incredulously. "As in, you can break my arm but don't break my leg? That kind of mercy?"

"No." He stared at me helplessly.

"Out with it, asshole." Jett was growing impatient like I was.

"I made a mistake," he said. "With Katarina. She won't talk to me, she won't look at me, and I've been completely cut out of her life."

"And I'm supposed to care because...?" I raised an eyebrow.

"Because I love her. She's been my friend since I made my first memory. I know my behavior toward her was wrong. I admit that—completely. I got carried away and a little crazed. I just wanted her so much and I was willing to do anything to make it happen. First, Ethan swooped her off her feet then you..." He shrugged. "Now I understand I need to let it go. She and I are never going to happen. But I really want her friendship back."

"I hate your guts so I don't understand why you're telling me this."

"Because I'm hoping you'll be willing to help me..."

Jett and I exchanged a look then we both started laughing.

"Good one," Jett said.

"I haven't heard such a good joke in a long time," I said as I dabbed at the moisture that pooled in my eyes.

Joey looked at the ground and his shoulders sagged. "Look, I love her and you love her. Please help me. I may not have been a good friend to her lately but I was before this. She misses me even if she won't admit it."

"I really don't think she does, man."

"Please." He pleaded with his eyes. "Do you have any idea how hard it was for me to come to you and ask for help?"

"It's pretty pathetic," Jett said.

"But I don't care about my pride because I want Katarina's friendship back."

"How do I know this isn't a ploy?" I asked. "Some plan to get her closer to you instead of me or some bullshit?"

"I guess you don't," he said. "But you really think Katarina would even look at me that way? It's pretty clear she's in love with you, just like she used to be with Ethan. I'm never going to come between that. I'm not a threat to you."

"But you went out of your way to dig dirt on me."

"And look where that got me," he said sadly. "Katarina won't even see me anymore."

There was no reason to pity him, but for some reason, I did. This guy was in love with the same woman I was in love with, but he couldn't have her. What would I have done if Katarina hadn't given me the time of day? If I loved her with everything I had but she refused to even glance my way? But that wasn't the only reason I pitied him. Losing a friend was hard, and even though I never saw the good times between them, Katarina did defend him at one point. So she did care about him. "I'll only do it under one condition."

His eyes lit up like the Fourth of July. "Anything."

"You never, ever pull this again. If you do, my boys and me will take you to a shipping dock and beat you to an inch of your life. Then we'll throw you in the harbor and watch you drown. Do we understand each other?"

"Yes...but does that still apply if you break up?"

My eyes narrowed on his face.

"Of course it does...yes, I understand."

"Are you sure?"

"Yes," he said quickly. "I miss my friend."

***

I entered Katarina's office first. "Male gigolo at your service." I walked inside, striding like I owned the room and everything in it. A cocky smile was on my face. "What are you into?"

She looked at me with that smile I loved. "A foot massage would be great."

"As in, you would massage my dick with your feet?"

She chucked her pen at me and laughed. "You're ridiculous."

"So...is that a yes?" I asked as I caught the pen.

"No." She ignored her paperwork and looked at me. "What are you doing here? I don't take lunch for at least another two hours."

"My dick missed you."

She gave me an incredulous look. "Your dick just saw me an hour ago."

"Yeah...he's a bit clingy."

She laughed and shook her head. "Babe, I have a lot of things to do today. I don't really have time to banter back and forth with you. It can wait until I get off work."

"Milkshake, we both know I don't wait for anything." I winked at her.

She grabbed another pen and threw it at me.

I caught it like last time. "Actually, there's something important I want to talk about."

That got her attention. "Okay. Is everything alright?"

"Yeah, everything is fine." I sat at the edge of her desk and looked down at her.

"So...?" She was eager to get through this conversation.

"Joey came by my apartment after you left."

Confusion set into her face first then anger followed quickly behind it. "What? Why?"

"He told me he's sorry for the way he acted and he really wants to be your friend again—a real friend."

She shook her head vigorously. "Friends don't blackmail each other."

"But he didn't tell anyone about me. And he's had weeks to do it."

She gave me a look full of fury. "Are you on his side? Last time I checked, you hated him."

"I do—I did. But he seems genuinely sorry."

"You don't strike me as a forgiving person."

"I'm not," I agreed. "But I remember the way you used to defend him. When I went to that diner to watch him, you were really upset. It was clear you really cared about him like family."

"Well, that was then. This is now." She leaned back in her chair and crossed her legs.

"He said he's sorry and wants your friendship back. He'll never try to get something more. He finally accepts you'll never be his."

She stared at a painting on her wall.

"He's outside if you want to talk to him face-to-face."

"He's here?" she hissed.

"He's practically family to you. Let's just get through this and move on. If he pulls anything again, I'll break all his limbs. I promise."

"That trust will never be there again."

"He understands that," I said. "He just wants your friendship. Listen to his apology and we'll go from there."

"I really don't understand why you're sticking your neck out for him."

I crossed my arms over my chest and released a deep sigh. "This is about you, not me. My hatred toward him is irrelevant. And you already lost one family member. I don't want you to lose another if he's really sorry."

She turned back to me with new eyes. The fury seemed to evaporate and now it was replaced by consideration.

Only I could pull that off. "You'll see him?"

She nodded. "I guess."

"Great." I leaned down and kissed her forehead before I opened her office door. "She'll see you now."

Joey jumped out of his chair then straightened his tie. He looked terrified, far more scared than when I showed up at that diner with my guys. He adjusted his tie again even though it was perfectly straight.

"Stop acting like a girl." I pushed him inside the office.

Joey walked inside and stopped when he spotted Katarina behind her desk. Then he took a deep breath before he sat in the chair facing her. He swallowed the lump in his throat and I could visibly see it.

I leaned against the wall and crossed my arms over my chest.

Joey eyed me, like he was surprised I was staying.

"I'm not going anywhere," I said darkly. "I may be giving you another chance but that doesn't mean I trust you."

Joey looked away and didn't make an argument.

"Proceed." I crossed my ankles.

Katarina stared at Joey blankly, not willing to speak first.

Joey fidgeted with his hands before he cleared his throat. "I'm sorry for my behavior. It was unacceptable and wrong. When I blackmailed you...it was terrible. But I never went through with it. I hope that counts for something."

"Not really," she said.

Joey flinched noticeably; taking the hit like it was physical. "This doesn't justify what I did, but...I'm just crazy in love with you. Ethan came around and swept you off your feet. Then when Cato made an appearance, I didn't want to lose you a second time. I was desperate. I realize now how wrong that was. I'd really like to be your friend, and only your friend, if you can find the strength to forgive me for what I've done." He looked at her with apologetic eyes, pleading to her.

Katarina grabbed a pen from her desk and spun it in her fingers. She held her silence, like she was thinking deeply. "And what if I had gave in to your demands? What if I had stopped seeing Cato and started dating you because I was forced to? You would have gone through with it without looking back. The only reason why you're apologizing and settling for my friendship is because you lost."

"No," he said weakly. "I wouldn't have done that. Seeing the sadness in your face every time you looked at me would have quickly changed my mind. I wanted you to be happy with me. If that wasn't possible, I wouldn't have forced it."

"I'd like to believe you but there's no way to really know." She continued to spin the pen in her fingers.

"I guess..." He shrugged. "I'm not asking you to trust me or treat me the way you used to. I understand our friendship will be different from this point onward. I'm okay with that. I just want to start over. In time, I'll convince you that you can trust me. I want you to be happy with whomever you love. Even if you and Cato broke up, I wouldn't pursue you—never again."

That seemed to catch Katarina's notice. "Really?"

"Truly," he said. "I intend to move on and see other women. I'm sure there's the perfect girl out there for me. But I'm not going to find her if I'm constantly pursuing a woman who's unavailable."

Katarina turned to me and gauged my reaction.

I nodded slightly.

Then she turned back to Joey. "Okay...I will tolerate you. For now. If I think you're being honest, then our friendship will grow. That's all I can give you."

He released a deep sigh. "I'll take it. Thank you." His shoulders relaxed and his breathing returned to normal. "If you aren't doing anything for lunch, you want to grab something to eat?" He quickly turned to me. "Cato as well."

"Sure," I said before Katarina could speak. "Sounds like a good idea."

***

When Katarina came home from work, she kicked off her heels and threw her purse on the table. Then she gave me a hard kiss like she did every day. "Missed you."

"Really? I just saw you a few hours ago."

"Well, I did." Her arms were around my neck and she looked up at me with adoration.

"Well, why wouldn't you miss me? Come on, look at me."

She rolled her eyes but her smile didn't fall. "You're so full of yourself it's unbelievable."

"I'm just confident."

"No, you're cocky."

"But you like me that way, right?"

She held me closer. "I love you that way."

"That's what I thought." I pulled away and grabbed her hand. "Follow me. I want to show you something."

"Ooh...what is it?"

"You'll see." We walked into the bedroom then I faced her against the wall where a white vanity sat. It had a small stool and a jewelry box sat on top. The mirror was vintage, made in the 1920's. On the surface was the picture of us skydiving. I snatched it from her apartment last time I was there.

"What's this?" She sat in the stool and felt the surface. She opened all the drawers then looked at herself in the mirror. "It's gorgeous, Cato. Where did you find it?"

"I made it," I said. "Except the mirror."

She gave me a surprised look. "You made this?"

"I used to work construction when I was younger. I know a few things." I loved seeing the excited look on her face. She clearly loved it.

"It's beautiful. I love it." She touched the jewelry box then turned back to me. "It was very thoughtful of you."

I kneeled beside her and looked into her face. "Move in with me."

Surprise came over her face. "What...?"

"Move in with me. This is your first piece of furniture." I patted the surface while I stared at her.

"Cato..."

"I'm not asking you. I'm telling you. I want to see you every day when I come home. I want to sleep with you every night. I want us to be together all the time. When I'm not with you, I miss you. Now say yes."

Her eyes watered and a smile overcame her face.

"I would ask you to marry me instead if I wasn't afraid it was too soon for you."

Her eyes watered more. "You want to get married?"

"What do you think?" I asked seriously. "I've been chasing you down like animal control with a butterfly net. You're the one, baby."

She cupped my face and kissed me. "I do want to get married."

I looked into her eyes and saw her sincerity. "You do?"

She nodded.

"It's not too soon?"

"No. Time is irrelevant. I married Ethan after two months and I have no regrets."

"I thought you might say that." I opened the drawer to her jewelry box. Inside sat a platinum ring with a large two-carrot diamond in the center.

She covered her mouth and gasped when she saw it.

"Marry me."

She continued to stare at the ring in shock.

I grabbed it then slipped it on her left hand. "Perfect fit."

She looked down at it as the tears started to pour. "Yes."

"I didn't ask, baby." I smiled at her. "I just told you to marry me."

She chuckled even though her face was red and wet. "Then I don't have a choice, do I?"

"No. You never had a choice."

Katarina

We stood outside the door together. I held a green bean casserole and Cato had his arm around my waist. I didn't knock. Instead, I looked down at the dish I prepared and hoped everyone would like it.

"Don't be nervous," he said. "There's no reason to be nervous."

"Well, I've never done this before..."

"They wouldn't have invited us if they didn't want us around—especially me."

"Yeah..." I knew he was right.

Cato waited for me to knock on the door. When I didn't, he did it himself. "Showtime."

My heart beat like a drum.

Cindy opened the door with wide eyes and excitement. "You're here." She hugged me hard while she moved around the dish in my hands. "So excited to see you, dear."

"I made a casserole," I blurted, feeling awkward.

"That was very thoughtful of you. Thank you." She took the dish then turned to Cato. "Wow, this is him?"

"Yeah," I said nervously.

"You have excellent taste in men, honey." Cindy pulled Cato in for a hug. "It's wonderful to meet you. Please come in and make yourself at home."

"Thank you," he said as he returned the embrace. "I'm Cato."

"Oh, I know who you are." She smiled as she pulled away. "I'm Cindy."

"It's a pleasure to meet you," Cato said.

Cindy spotted my left hand. "Oh my! I'm blind!"

I smiled then held up my hand. "Cato did a good job."

"It's beautiful," she said as she examined it. "And I'm so happy for you." She gave me a look that showed her sincerity. "So very happy for you."

Cato shot me a look that said, "Told you so."

"Come in," Cindy said as she escorted us inside. "Jim is eager to see you. He's been talking about you all day."

We entered the house then moved into the dining area.

"There she is!" Jim gave me a smile I'd known for years then hugged me tightly, almost with too much force. "Pretty like always."

"Thanks, Jim. It's nice to see you." I turned to Cato. "Let me introduce my...fiancé." I wasn't used to saying that word.

Cato extended his hand. "It's a pleasure to meet you, sir."

Jim ignored his hand and hugged him instead. "The pleasure is all mine, boy." He clapped his shoulder and stepped back. "Welcome to the family."

"It's been a very warm welcome," Cato said politely.

Gabe came next and introduced himself. "Dang, I was hoping Katarina would end up with me. But I'm a graceful loser." He fist-bumped Cato.

"You can't win them all, right?" Cato said playfully.

"Dinner is ready," Cindy called from the table.

"Make sure you eat everything," I said to Cato. "If not, Cindy will shove it down your throat."

Cato chuckled. "Thanks for the warning."

We gathered around the table and began to eat.

I thought it would be weird to bring a new man to Ethan's parents house. They'd always been family to me, even during the years when Ethan was gone. They treated me like their daughter the moment I crossed over the threshold. And they treated me the same now. The happiness on their faces was obvious. They were glad I was happy and no longer mournful.

Cato didn't seem uncomfortable. He got along with everyone well, and made Gabe laugh several times. Cindy kept complimenting my ring and asking about our wedding plans. We hadn't talked about anything because we were enjoying being engaged for the moment.

When we finished eating, Cindy suddenly turned serious. "We're so happy you found someone to share your life with. And we all know Ethan is happy too."

Their blessing meant a lot to me. I loved their son with my whole heart when he was alive. But five years had come and gone, and living in constant mourning wasn't really living. Cato broke down my walls and taught me how to love again. And now I was happier than I'd been in a really long time. Knowing I had the support of everyone around me, including Ethan, was what I needed more.

Cato turned to me with a smile on his face.

"And we'll have lots of babies," I said. "Just like Ethan wanted."

Dark Escort

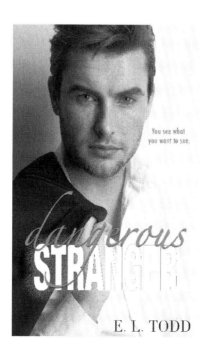

book four of the beautiful entourage series

dangerous STRANGER

Jett & Ophelia

AVAILABLE NOW

You see what
you want to see.

E. L. TODD

Show Your Support

Like E. L. Todd on Facebook:

https://www.facebook.com/ELTodd42?ref=hl

Follow E. L. Todd on Twitter:

@E_L_Todd

Subscribe to E. L. Todd's Newsletter:

www.eltoddbooks.com

Other Books by
E. L. TODD

Alpha Series

Sadie

Elisa

Layla

Janet

Cassie

Hawaiian Crush Series

Connected By The Sea

Breaking Through The Waves

Connected By The Tide

Taking The Plunge

Riding The Surf

Laying in the Sand

Forever and Always Series

Only For You

Forever and Always

Edge of Love

Force of Love

Fight For Love

Lover's Roulette
Happily Ever After
The Wandering Caravan
Come What May
Again and Again
Lover's Road
Meant To Be
Here and Now
Until Forever
New Beginnings
Love Conquers All
Love Hurts
The Last Time
Sweet Sins
Lost in Time
Closing Time

Southern Love

Then Came Alexandra
Then Came Indecision
Then Came Absolution
Then Came Abby
Abby's Plight

Printed in Great Britain
by Amazon